NICKY FACES CATASTROPHE... AND SURVIVES?!

MATTI MCLEAN

Spectrum Books

Contents

This book is dedicated to anyone who needs a laugh right about now. Because damn.

PROLOGUE

The forest was quiet. It twinkled brilliantly in the starlight as the harvest moon radiated down upon the sacred forest grove. There, all the fae were gathered as the great chieftain took to his placement at the front. Surely this would quell the uprising. Surely this would fix the world. He raised his hands reverently and a great hush fell over the crowds of pixies, fairies, fae and demons that surrounded the sacred grove.

"We are gathered here today to edify our elders," the great tree chieftain cried as he lifted his thick wooden arms above the assembled crowds. "We all know how the forces of Donn have been gaining power, and together with him being joined by the Fae king and queen, we are all in, like, seriously deep shit."

A murmur bubbled up amongst the inhabitants of the forest.

"Alas, poor us!"

"Hark! This is like, really bad you guys!"

"Doesn't she fucking hate him?" A small, impish pixie called out. The tree elder looked upon it. It was so cute the great chieftain could hardly stand it. He wanted to eat it - but did not as he was an elder, and eating the pixies was considered uncouth. He brushed his long grassy hair out of his face and lifted the floral sceptre above the crowd again. He looked like a boss. This was because he was.

"We all must be unified if we are to preserve our lineage from the great reckoning which is to come."

"Yeah? And how do we do that?" another pixie squeaked. This one was covered in mud and mushrooms. He was much easier to ignore because he was ugly.

"I have taken it upon myself to add an addition to our druid bloodline. A mortal who can come alongside our brethren and fight for us in the coming war."

The grove grew silent. This was forbidden. This was blasphemy. This was - like - the worst.

"Yo... What?" a reddish demon squawked.

The wooden fae leader whisked his arms aside, revealing a tallish man with brown hair and excessively white skin. "Friends of the forest, meet Keith."

"Howdy y'all. My name is Keith and I want to join your cause." For once, the Fae of the forest were still. None said anything as Keith waved at them like a doofus. Either he didn't understand what he was doing there, or he didn't comprehend the gravity of where he was.

"He doesn't look like a very good choice!" a frog exclaimed from the back.

"He doesn't look very smart!" a bat cried out from the sky.

"Are you legit shitting us? I mean, come on!"

Soon the entire forest grove was raucous chaos, with poor, awkward, extremely human Keith in the centre of things, not understanding where he was or what was going on. To be fair, that was par for the course with Keith. At the best of times, his name was Keith, so he was expected to have a hard life—but this felt more personal than that.

"I think y'all need to stop yelling so I can hear what it is that you've all got going on," Keith tried to reply, but the wave of boos levelled at him was exceptionally loud.

The crowd grew heavy in their discontent and began to close in on the forest tree.

"I am the forest chieftain! I have already blessed this man with divine insight! He shall carry it through his bloodline for a thousand years and be the father of many a mortal warrior!" He exclaimed, but it was too late. The forest glen had descended into chaos as the spirits left the community to go out and fend for themselves.

"You think Donn is still hiring?" The sweet pixie asked.

"Who the fuck cares? Gotta be better than here," a ghost whispered back as he floated away.

"Stop! Wait! You cannot go out there! Come back! Now!" The chieftain had lost control, and he knew it. He grabbed the sacred book and grit his wooden teeth together. He knew he mustn't use it, for the evils within were savage and dangerous. But he was tempted. Within moments, the grove had cleared, leaving only the chieftain and stupid Keith resting in there.

"Well, shucks." Keith finally spoke after a long, stunned silence.

The Chieftain looked at him sadly and then retreated back into the woods he had come from.

Some would say that Keith was the bringer of the end. Some thought that he was the great evil that was prophesied that would destroy the Fae world. But none could argue that he was a silly, piffling trifle of a man.

With no choice, the Chieftain was forced to expel the dreaded Keith into the real world, but left the blessing intact. No one knew what this would mean for the coming reckoning, but at the very least, his offspring would be some of the most important in the universe.

Or maybe they wouldn't be.

Chapter 1

THE CHAPTER WHERE NICKY TAKES A SHOWER

Even if nothing else in his life was going right, Nicky knew that he'd always have job security working at a video rental store. If he stayed the course, he'd have free video rentals for the rest of his life. Which, if he kept to his modern diet, would allow him to live until he was at least thirty-five.

With the grace of a snake unhinging its jaw, he took a bite of his ham sandwich, lightly drowned in mustard, and gazed at his television screen- a full fourteen inches of glorious full colour that weighed the same as him. On it, a buxom blonde in a skimpy dress purred at a man in a trench coat and lopsided fedora. The woman was beautiful. The man was handsome. He didn't particularly care for either, but he liked the hat. He always liked hats.

The movie itself wasn't amazing. He wasn't sure what they were saying as he'd forgotten to pay attention when it started, but at least they seemed highly invested in each other. Chomping the last of the sandwich, he put one hand in his pants, the other butting out the last embers of his joint and laid back, exhaling a thick plume of smoke into his 'highly unique' basement apartment. He didn't have anyone to impress today, and if he didn't have to put on pants, all the better.

He blinked. He wasn't sure if he was high, sleepy or evaporating but was rocketed back into reality when the woman screamed. Nicky jumped and tried to focus his blurry mind on the screen. Maybe she was being murdered or something, but he couldn't tell. The main character murdering her would've made for a good movie. He definitely wouldn't have seen that coming. He'd have to watch this again soon. Whatever it was.

He blinked again, and the credits rolled. Nicky slouched forwards and rolled onto the ground like a poorly animated pancake. With a yawn, he ambled his way into the kitchen. It wasn't a nice kitchen, obviously, but he did his best to keep it well stocked with the essentials: cheesy poofs, pop-tarts, soda, beer, and mustard. Sometimes he even had mayo.

Fortunately for him, more and more of his days were turning into lazy days. With no real friends outside of his work circle and no prospective dates in the future, he didn't feel compelled to make any effort regarding his appearance. His face unshaven, his hair wild and unkempt, and a soft settling of pudge gripping to his frame just enough for all his clothes to look uncomfortable and undersized. Luckily for him, he didn't mind any of this. Being lazy just meant fewer people expected anything from him.

He opened the door to the fridge, which fell off the hinges, and gently crushed his toe. This happened every time he opened it and as a result, he had long ago lost all feeling in it. He grabbed a warm beer from the warm fridge and cracked it open, sending a shower of foam over his hands and face. With a curse, he put it down on the counter and started to lick it off himself like a cat. Some might consider this uncouth, but he wasn't about to waste mediocre beer. His mother had paid for it, after all.

RING!

As he attempted to lick his elbow, his eyes shot over to the avocado-coloured phone on the wall. With a grunt, he shuffled over to it and picked up the receiver. It normally had a cord that could extend out of his apartment, across the street, down the block and back- but the cord was now balled into a tangle so intense, Nicky could barely hold it a foot away from the wall. Cuddling into his wall like a gecko, he softly pressed himself into plaster and cleared his throat to sound human.

"Hello?" Nicky grumbled. He did not sound human.

"Hey Nicky!" The shrill, happy voice sent his eyes rolling back into his head so hard he could see his thoughts. It was his mother. "Nicky! Baby! Nicky! It's your mom!" she exclaimed, as if he could have forgotten her.

He tried to suppress it, but the groan was inevitable. He loved his mom, but much like an amorous gorilla, her love was best experienced from afar.

"Very nice Nick Nick. You know me. It's your mom. The one that birthed you?" His mom was the only person he knew who pronounced birthed as a three-syllable word.

"Hi mom," he said, trying to sound chipper. It came out more like a woodchipper.

"You need to smile when you talk to me on the phone. It makes your voice better."

Nicky loved his mom. But there were moments where he would rather run naked through a cornfield than talk to her.

"Is this better?" he asked through grit teeth.

"So much. Hey Nicky! I wanted to know if you wanted to

come by today. Bill and I are going shopping, so we won't be home from one until six, but you can come before or after. But definitely come by for six. Okay, baby? Will we see you then?" His hands clenched the phone a bit tighter. He could hear a spritzing sound as his mom drenched her head in hairspray. He could almost smell it through the phone.

"You want me to come by today?"

"Only if you want to, baby. But listen! I'm going to be done after six, okay? It's just a bit of shopping, but I really need to get it done and Bill is just such a help with it all. Come by for dinner after? Would you like that baby?" Nicky sighed.

"Will Bill be there?"

"Of course! Why wouldn't Bill be here? He lives here! He says a-hi by the way."

"Look, I'm a bit..."

"What do you have against Bill?" Her voice went from saccharine sweet to lemon sour in an instant.

"I don't..."

"Look, you be here at the right time, now 'k? Six. On the dot." The tone left Nicky no ability to argue. In frustration, he gently kicked the wall. If his toe was capable of feeling things still, he would have squealed. Sometimes he was amazed it didn't just fall off him. He squeezed at his temples as if massaging them off his face.

"Look, I'll come by around eight if you..."

"Oh goody," the sweet tone cooed. "Seven. You're such a good son sometimes. Okay, baby! I'll see you later then! Okay! Buh bye! Bye bye now. Bill! He said..." The dial tone blared, but it took Nicky a moment to realise the sound wasn't his mother droning on. He exhaled. He lumbered back to his beer and took a swig, and lamented his lost day. He'd actually have to clean himself up today. Even worse, he'd have to wear pants.

At least he still had time to drink. He took the beer into the bathroom and precariously balanced it on the back of the toilet. Stripping down, he caught a glimpse of himself in the dirty mirror and frowned. He had a good three days' worth of stubble, and his toothbrush looked more like a dog toy than a hygienic tool. He didn't want to go to the dentist, but he knew that eventually he'd have to in order to discover just how damaged his teeth were—but if he didn't have any left, then he wouldn't have to worry about that... It was good to have options.

While he was nothing special to look at, he didn't feel any pressure to look better than he did. His body was soft, but he still had some muscle underneath from when he'd played sports long ago. His hair was dark and shaggy, but his eyes were a piercing green, which gave him a mysterious quality. Specifically, how can such a garbage hurricane of a human have such nice eyes?

With the grace of an elephant high jumping, he stepped into the shower and turned the tap. The faucet vomited up a thick stream of tepid grey water to blast out of the rusty head. It smelled like dirt, which was better than it normally did. Thankfully, he had soap this time, so that was a good sign. He poured a healthy portion of what he hoped was shampoo into his meaty paw and lathered it through his greasy locks. He swore he could feel some of the hairs leaving his scalp as he rubbed, but he was in his late twenties and unlucky, so he was just thankful it was hanging in there at all.

With a trepidatious glance out of the shower, he peered at the grimy mirror and looked up at his scalp for any sign of a bald patch. He may not have been the most attractive man, but at least he had enough sense to be vain about his hairline. As he did, a dollop of shampoo wormed its way into his eye. The sting was monumental and instantaneous - and Nicky let out a yelp of pain as he tried to gather enough dirty water in his hands to scrub it out.

Then the doorbell rang and his shower plunged from a decent heat to Arctic beach. The drop in temperature was so rapid that he spiralled into his shower curtain, colliding with the wall and the floor in that order. Shampoo now cascaded down his face and into his eyes, searing it as only tear-free shampoo can. A blotch of red appeared and he could smell the scent of blood linger in his nostrils. Letting out a string of profanities, he unwrapped himself from his shower curtain, grabbed a towel that he hoped would cover most of him. He awkwardly stumbled through his bathroom and swung open the door. Apparently not knowing his own strength, the door flew off the hinges and landed with a thud in the middle of his living room.

The doorbell rang again, this time causing all the lights in his basement to flicker.

"I'm coming!" He let out a guttural yell as he staggered through the apartment, tripping over the bathroom door on the way, and adhering the towel to himself as best he could. He flung open the front door, clearing as much of the soapy mess out of his face as he could. He probably looked more like a beast with a head full of blood and shampoo and a scowl on his face, eager to tear apart whatever he came across. Thankfully, standing outside his apartment was his friend, Teddy.

"Hey, Nicky." Teddy was one of those guys who had a new job every week. Pleasant enough, but the type of white person who thought that mayo was a spice. His short brown hair and blue eyes made him look clean cut and boring, but deep down, he actually was.

"Teddy? What are you-?"

"You got a package." Nicky paused before looking down and crossing his legs. "No... a package." Teddy held a small package wrapped in brown paper in his hands and tried not to make eye contact.

"Ah! Yes. Quite." He said as he grabbed the package from Teddy and manoeuvred it inside without letting the towel drop from his nether region. "Do I need to sign for it or..."

"Yeah. Here," Teddy said, as he gave him a clipboard. Nicky then looked from it, to the towel, to the package, to his package and tried to work out how he was supposed to sign for it. Nicky gripped the pen in his teeth and wobbled it feebly on the page.

"Doing this now?" Nicky asked as he tried not to inhale the pen.

"Yeah. For now. We'll see," Teddy replied, his voice as excited as tapioca. "You still at-"

"Mideo Video? Yeah."

"You really like it there, huh?"

"It's good for what I want to do."

"Oh yeah? What's that?" Teddy asked.

"Nothing at all. Thanks for the package." Nicky backed his way into the house, but Teddy stopped him.

"Hey, if you ever want to grab a brew or something, I'm just down the street."

"Yeah. I mean... yeah," he said as he slowly backed up into the room and nodded a quick goodbye to his friend. "Let's catch up sometime when I'm not naked."

Nicky closed the door and gazed at the package in his hand. He wasn't sure who had sent it, or what it was, or why he should want it, but a free package was a free package and the siren call of the mystery was too strong.

Whatever was inside of it was special. It was magical.

But first he realised he should probably stop the bleeding.

Chapter 2

The Chapter Where Things Start To Happen

Lucky for him, blood was something he had in abundance. And the fact that he had seen so much of it and only passed out twice was promising.

Once he was wearing pants and ready for the day, he returned to the table and eyed the package like it was a fresh fruitcake. Curious and tempting, but why was it here in the first place?

By all measures, it was a package. Just an ordinary package. But this was no ordinary package. How could it be when he had received it? People didn't send him things unless it was a cease-and-desist letter or an oversized letter with hundreds of stamps inside, where you could buy hundreds of musical albums for only a dollar. One day he aspired to be able to afford that dollar, but for now he had bigger problems.

A strange package from a strange someone sitting in the middle of his kitchen table- like a duck would if it happened to want to. He frowned at it. He glared at it. He peered at it, but couldn't decipher anything interesting about it.

Though not a scholar, he read and re-read the address many times. It was definitely for him. It was definitely a box, and it definitely had his name on it. He could verify this. He stroked his chin as if maybe doing so would reveal secrets about what he would need to do next. But alas, his chin was no help. It was a stupid chin, anyway.

Pressing his hands on the table, he leaned in close to try to find something that he missed. He found nothing. No tears. No funny stickers. No jury duty tags- With no other options, he did the only thing he could think of and began the process of opening it. Peeling the sides of the brown paper box back, he saw what looked like a smaller package inside.

The second layer was much like the first, but this layer was covered in drawings and words. Things like, 'Don't open', 'Seriously, don't open', 'Danger inside', 'For the love of god don't open' and, 'Why are you still reading this? Untold horrors inside. Opening could lead to the destruction of all mankind. Don't fucking open it. Don't even think about it.' He scratched at his chin again. He wondered if it meant anything.

Despite the urging on the paper, Nicky peeled back the wrapping to find something unexpected. There, in the middle of the wrapping, sitting innocently on his kitchen table, was a book. It was a big book and appeared to be very old, with a thick leather cover and strange symbols and writings all over it. Simply having an actual book in his home was strange enough, but this one looked fancy and expensive. This looked like a book that didn't just have pictures of nude people inside either—it looked like it would contain actual words. It's a well-known fact that you couldn't watch a book, so Nicky had little use for the dead medium. But having a book in his house just looked unnatural. Out of place. On some level, it scared him.

Cautiously, he sat in his chair and leaned over the book. He touched it. He smelled it. He would have licked it, but that would involve him moving closer, which didn't seem worth the effort.

The more he examined it, the more he became convinced that this was indeed a book. He wasn't sure what he expected, but it felt like paper, looked like paper, and, presumably, it tasted like paper. For a moment, Nicky questioned when he had last held something that wasn't plastic, or food, or himself—and couldn't recall. With a shrug, he slid the book in front of him and exhaled. With a steady hand, he opened it.

From there, it was like someone had turned on the dark. A tsunami of sludge erupted from the book like a firehose of oil, or a really bad reaction to Indian food. A vortex of black erupted from the book like Satan's ejaculate. It felt as if reality was ripping the skin off of his face as a flood of energy pinned him against his chair.

Fighting the forces that pinned him down, he reached out to try to close the book, but the torrent coming from it made getting close to it impossible. Nicky extended his arm out, feeling the silky smooth substance blast through his outstretched fingers. Everything smelled foul, and he felt like he'd been submerged in a volcano of lubricant, but to his surprise, it didn't flood his apartment. Instead, the substance seemed to blast straight through the walls without leaving a mark.

For a moment, Nicky wondered if he was drowning. He couldn't breathe. The air around him was thick with oil. The world itself was wailing with a fury he could hardly comprehend. It was like he was back working in fast food. Just when he thought he was going to die, something happened.

There was a bang as his front door flew open, and for a moment, he wondered if Teddy had come in for a chat. But it wasn't the gentle minded plain bagel of a man he had expected. When Nicky looked up, he saw a strange man in black clothing standing over him with a flaming sword and an amazing body. Nicky quickly realised that he did not know this person.

The man leapt to his side and grabbed Nicky by the shoulder. With a yank, he pulled him back, away from the energy blasting out of the book. Nicky skidded across the floor and collided with the fridge. As was expected, the door fell off once again and lovingly landed on top of him.

Nicky watched as the man took the long, flaming sword, wedged it under the book, and with a flick of his wrist, closed it without any resistance. As he did, the energy blast ceased, and the man turned to Nicky with a grimace on his face. The man was unquestionably handsome, with a rough and distinct look about him. He looked savage and angry.

Nicky pointed to his front door, barely hanging onto its hinges.

"You're paying for that," he said. The man glared at him and ripped the black scarf off his face. He raised his sword and swooped down in front of Nicky, pinning him with his vicious gaze.

"Can you not read?" He sounded angry.

"You sound angry."

"I asked you a question. Can you read or not?"

"I can read." Nicky shrugged.

"And all those warnings on the package? And the book? You just ignored them?" the man growled.

"I thought they were just suggestions? Like do not open, or don't eat the mushrooms." The man blinked at him. He gestured dramatically to the book and to the thin layer of black oil that now coated his entire apartment.

"You just unleashed a series of demons. A Kelpie. A

Bauchan. A Dullahan!"

"Gesundheit." The man gripped Nicky by the throat and lifted him off the ground. He didn't even struggle. Nicky clenched onto his wrist in an attempt to breathe, but was finding it hard to do so.

"You stupid piece of human trash," the man growled. "Do you even have any concept of what you've just done?" He relinquished his grip and Nicky fell to the floor. Nicky coughed a few times before staggering to his feet as the stranger paced the room.

"That hurt, you know. It's not nice to choke someone in their own home." Nicky coughed. The man ignored him as he stomped back and forth. "What are you doing?"

"I'm thinking! Pacing helps me think!" the stranger said.

"No. I mean like here. In my house. Can you think outside?" The man froze. With wide-eyed fury, he turned his full attention to Nicky. Nicky flicked his hands a couple times in a shoo motion to make his point clear.

Raising up to his full height, which was taller than Nicky at least, he sheathed his sword. He gritted his teeth and stormed to the table. Nicky ran to him and blocked the man from getting there first.

"What are you doing?" Nicky asked.

"Grabbing the book before you unleash another horrible monstrosity on the world," he said through his perfect clenched teeth. Nicky frowned at him. Sure, the book had unleashed something weird, but it was his book. It had been delivered to him. He wasn't going to let some stranger take something that was clearly meant for him. Was this selfish? Yes. Did it matter? Maybe.

"You can't take that," Nicky said.

"I have to," the stranger retorted. "You've already caused enough trouble with it."

"But it was addressed to me. It means someone must have sent it."

"It wasn't meant for you, idiot. It was meant for the next in the bloodline of Keith, and clearly...." Nicky'd had enough. He grabbed the book and was planning to jump over the table to put an obstacle between him and the man. What actually happened was as soon as he touched the book, he was frozen in place. He attempted to lift it up, but it wouldn't move. He grunted as he tried to will his body to do anything, but he was stuck.

"What the hell are you doing?" the man asked. He sounded tired.

"Outrunning you! As soon as... I just need..." he grunted as he attempted to move the book away, but he couldn't move his feet. He could lift the book, but wasn't able to walk anywhere. He wasn't moving. He felt like a fish in a toaster. He looked from the book to the man, back to the book, and back to the man, and then, for good measure, back to the book again. Then he looked to the man's sword and calculated his chances of being able to run away. They didn't look promising, but thankfully he was bad at math. This man looked like he not only thought swords were cool, but knew how to use them.

"Put the book down. Before it bonds with you," the man said. Nicky sighed. It was a stupid idea, anyway.

"Fine! You win! Take the book," Nicky said. His body loosened, and he was able to offer it to him. The man frowned at him and grabbed the book, but when he took it away, Nicky's hand severed from his wrist and went with it.

"Great. Now look what you've done." He shook his head. Nicky looked down at the stump where his hand had been seconds before and frowned.

"Oh," he replied. And then, as he looked from the wrist stump to the hand and back again, he began to scream.

Chapter 3

THE CHAPTER WHERE THEY'RE STUCK TOGETHER

Nicky wasn't sure how long he had been screaming, but it felt like an appropriate amount of time. He looked at his hand-less limb and waggled it in front of the man's face like it was an especially floppy fish. The man didn't appear impressed, but then again, Nicky wasn't exactly sure what he was try-ing to waggle when his hand was no longer attached to his wrist.

"If you don't stop right now, I will take this sword and shove it down your throat until you can't scream, or breathe, or do -it- like that anymore!" The man huffed. Nicky paused as he contemplated what the man had just said.

"That started out threatening but then..."

"It got away from me, okay?" The man lowered his sword and shook his head. "Now just... calm down. Can you do that?"

"Okay. Yes. I... I am fine," Nicky said after a moment. The man looked at him with a frown.

"Are you calm?"

"Why would I be calm?! My hand fell off!" The man shook his head in frustration.

"It didn't fall off. The book took it. Here." He gave Nicky the book and when he reached out his handless arm for it, his hand reconnected with his body. He put the book down, held his hand up and wiggled his fingers with a sense of amazement rarely felt outside of drugs. Feeling exhilarated by the reconnecting hand, he let out a howl of laughter.

"Oh, my god! My hand! It's back! I need this hand so badly you have no idea."

"I have some ideas." He said, rolling his crystalline eyes. Nicky was struck for a moment by the man's long, luxurious eyelashes. They looked a little too perfect to be real.

"I just need it too..."

"I get it. Just... don't." The man said as Nicky made a lewd gesture towards his personal area.

"I just... it feels so good to have it back. That's all." He smiled at the man and brushed his hands on his pants. He then stretched up and smiled as he ushered towards the door. "Cool. Thanks for giving me my hand back, but you can go now." The man didn't move. Then he blinked at Nicky very deliberately as if saying something with his eyes. His face was cold and stone-like. Nicky wondered if he'd stopped breathing. The man frowned—again. He seemed to do that a lot.

"After all that drama, you expect me to leave without the book?"

"Yeah. It's my book. It was sent to me. It took my hand. I'd say that's a clear sign that it wants to stay with me."

"You will give me that-"

"Buddy, I don't even know who you are. You expect me to trust someone when I don't even know their name?"

"I have no name," he said.

"Then you better come up with one." The man crossed his arms and glared at him. Nicky stood defiantly in front of the book, protecting it. The man shook his head in disbelief.

"Call me Will."

"Cool. Nice to meet you. Will. Now leave my house." Will clenched his handsome face into a frown, which Nicky was getting used to.

"I save your life, and you still try to kick me out?" he spat.

"Life is hard." Nicky shrugged. "Now leave."

"I'm not leaving without that book. Clearly you can't be trusted with it."

"You can't leave with it or you'll take my hand with you. And from what I understand, that would be bad." Will gripped his sword and slashed at Nicky, forcing him to stagger backwards into an open box of *Fluffy O Cereals*. The box was a poor support of his weight and he quickly toppled to the ground.

"I can take your hands with or without the book," Will said, taking a step toward Nicky with the sword in front of him. Nicky turned to run away but instead slammed straight into his kitchen counters which spilled more of the brightly coloured cereal all over the counter. He then turned back as Will pressed the tip of the sword into Nicky's chest.

"Come now, you don't need to stab me. You wouldn't want to do that, would you? Not to me! I'm your old friend Nicky!" Will raised the sword and pressed it into Nicky's throat. Nicky noticed for the first time that the sword has beautiful designs etched all over it. He hadn't appreciated its craftsmanship until it was preparing to skewer him like a meat popsicle.

"Look. Up until now, I've been nice. I've played along to your little game, but now is the time where I need you to start to cooperate with me. For whatever reason, this book has bonded to you and now we're both stuck with a very unpleasant reality that I'm not looking forward to."

"What- What do you mean?" Nicky asked, afraid of what was to come next. Will shook his head and lowered the sword as he disappeared into his thoughts.

"I have to work with you now." Will frowned.

"At Mideo Video? Look, Will, I just work there. I don't have any hiring abilities. I mean, I could talk to Vinny, but..."

"Shut up." Will pressed his sword and Nicky realised that if he'd wanted to, he could've sliced him in twain right then and there. Nicky was surprised by how much it hurt. He'd seen people hold swords to people's throats before in movies, but this actually hurt. If he wasn't careful, he could cut himself.

Then he sneezed.

Had Will not been an expert swordsman, he likely would have punctured his own throat, but luckily an expert swordsman was exactly what Will appeared to be.

"Idiot..." Will whispered.

"Can you hand me a tissue?" Nicky asked as he tried to wipe his nose. He was surprised how much mucus fell out, and it didn't appear to be stopping.

Will did not appear impressed, but from their interactions so far, that seemed par for the course. He took the flat edge of the sword and smacked Nicky's side, sending the snotty clod awkwardly stumbling into the middle of the room.

"You have five minutes to go and get changed before we hunt those things down. Capeesh?" Nicky looked at Will, confused, as he attempted to stop the avalanche dripping from his nostrils.

"We have to do the what with the where now?" Nicky asked.

"Just... we've got work to do. Go get dressed."

"So... Is this like a business casual type thing? I don't have much but I can..."

"You have five minutes, then we leave." Will raised the sword again in an attempt to silence Nicky. It worked. "Don't disappoint me." Then Will looked at the book and frowned. "Again."

Chapter 4

THE CHAPTER WHERE THEY FIGHT A THING

"I don't know how to dress if you won't tell me where we're going," Nicky whined. He had just emerged from the closet, which sometimes doubled as his bedroom, wearing torn jeans, mismatched socks and an old t-shirt that had a bottle of bleach on it called *Shine White Powder Clean*. Will looked at him.

"You have all your clothes to choose from and this is what you wear?" He frowned.

"They're the least dirty," Nicky said, sniffing them. "I think."

"Fine. Come on. Grab the book." Nicky looked at him.

"Why don't you grab the book? You're standing right there." Nicky pointed to him and then to the book as if to show how close together they were.

"I can't take the book. Not anymore. It's bonded with you. If I took it, I wouldn't be able to go anywhere. You need to grab the book." Nicky looked at the book again and frowned. This time, a shiver of panic rushed down his spine like it had just swallowed an ice cube. He looked at Will with a pout.

"But I don't want to grab the book." Will's mouth twitched.

"Why not?"

"Last time, my hand did the whole..." He motioned at his

hand and then waved it like it was floating away. Will rolled his eyes.

"Your point?"

"I don't like that."

"Just grab the book and follow me." Will left the place in a flourish and Nicky hesitated.

He eyed the book and felt a shiver. He contemplated finding an alternate exit, but considering he was underground and his front door was dangling precariously on its hinges, he realised he was trapped. Aside from that, he didn't want to burrow out like a mole as that would be too much effort and his squishy body wouldn't make it far. That and his apartment had no windows. That's what made burrito nights so dangerous.

Once Will was outside, Nicky walked over to the book and examined it. By all accounts it looked normal. Sure, he was no expert, but to his knowledge, this book looked like how a book should look. It had pages. It had a cover. But then he noticed there was no title. Even movie covers had titles on them. How would people know what they were supposed to watch if there was no title? Whomever made this book hadn't given much thought to their audience. Surely this was why the medium was dying.

His hand hovered above the book for a moment. Holding his breath, he swooped down and grabbed it like he was trying not to set off a trap. Then he was just holding the book in his hand, which to him felt unnatural. He carried it to the door expecting some kind of calamity, but only normality persisted. To his surprise, his hand didn't fly off and leave his body. He stepped out into the backyard expecting something terrible, like the apocalypse or a political rally. But there was nothing, only

Will sharpening his sword.

"My hand is fine, by the way," Nicky snarked. "It hasn't come off or anything."

"Congratulations. Where is your vehicle? We have to depart," Will asked without looking at him.

"My vehicle?"

"Your mode of transportation. Where is it?"

"Oh. I don't have one." Will's face puckered as if he had just swallowed a black hole.

"You don't have any mode of transport?"

Nicky shook his head. "I mean, I have shoes. Is that a bad thing?" Will clenched his jaw and flung his sword back in its sheath so hard Nicky was amazed it didn't snap off. "You've got a real anger problem there, friend. Be careful or you'll break something."

"I'd break your spine in half right now if I could, you detestable..." Will paused. He closed his eyes and took a deep breath. "Okay. You don't have a way to get there easily. That's fine."

"I try to be environmentally conscious with these things." Nicky quipped. Will smacked his lips.

"We will have to walk," Will said, turning his back to Nicky.

"Is it far? Should I wear my comfortable shoes then?" Will glared at him with the ferocity of a drunk lighthouse. "I'll get my comfortable shoes."

"You're wearing sneakers."

"But these are my rough sneakers. I'm going to grab my soft sneakers." Will looked like he wanted to say something, but didn't. Nicky assumed that was fine.

After a quick change into his walking shoes, they were off. Will walked quickly and Nicky had to trot just to keep up. A couple times, Nicky tried to double back, or to get away without Will noticing, but he always seemed to know where he was. It was like he had a fifth sense or something. He didn't like walking- and he especially didn't like having to walk carrying a book. It was heavy and awkward. What if one of his friends saw him carrying this? They might think he was a nerd, or worse—someone who read for fun. The thought chilled him to his jiggly core.

"Can you slow down at least?"

"I am going slow. You need to be faster."

"I'm going as fast as..." Will stopped and grabbed Nicky by the collar.

"You need to be faster. You're going to be hunting creatures bigger, faster and stronger than you ever imagined. You need to be fast. You need to be quick. You need to keep walking... and shut up." Nicky looked at him.

"I'm doing what now?" Will shook his head in response and pushed Nicky back. Nicky attempted to unwrinkle his already wrinkled shirt. He failed. "You're very forceful, you know that?"

"It's a feature, not a bug," Will retorted.

"You don't need to be so mean. You're very unlikeable," Nicky responded. Will turned purple.

"And you're an idiot! A dangerous idiot with a bomb in his pocket!" Will was so angry he appeared to be shaking. He then felt around his waist and pulled at the zipper of a small black fanny pack that he wore around his waist. Nicky had never noticed it before, but then again, he hadn't been looking at much of Will except for his wild and intense eyes. Will grabbed a small tube of lip chap and applied it angrily to his face before thrusting it back in the pouch with the same efficiency as sheathing his sword. Nicky could now confirm that Will was probably the coolest person he had ever encountered in his life.

"It's not a bomb. It's just a book."

"It's not just a book! It's a compendium!" Will yelled.

"Gesundheit," Nicky replied. Will yelled again as he stormed away.

"I shouldn't even be here! I shouldn't have to be babysitting the stupidest person to ever have the compendium in their possession!"

"I can't be the stupidest," Nicky retorted.

"Nope. You are. By far. You know how I know that? For two hundred years, no one else was stupid enough to open the damn thing!"

"Two hundred years? That can't be...-" His thought was interrupted when Nicky felt Will's hand clamp over his mouth. He felt himself being pulled behind the hedges of an overly manicured front lawn. The grass was very green. It was disconcerting.

Will guided Nicky, forcing him to kneel on the ground. Nicky felt Will kneel next to him and point to something in the road. Slowly, Nicky followed his gaze, and then he saw it.

"It's a stop sign!"

"Shut up and listen!" Will hissed.

Nicky closed his eyes. Then he heard it, but didn't realise what it was. The sound of hooves on asphalt was a bizarre combination, but as the large figure crept closer, he could hear it intensify. He opened his eyes to see a ghostly image approaching. A large black beast with long billowing fabric stretching far behind it. Straddling the form appeared to be most of a man dressed in long black robes, but it wasn't until he got where the head should be that he realised the figure didn't have one.

"What the fuck is that?" Nicky exclaimed. Will gripped him by the shoulder and hushed him.

"It'll hear you!"

"It's got no fucking head!" Nicky exclaimed. Will covered his mouth once again, but it was futile. "It can't hear us! It's got no head!"

"Idiot! Look what it's carrying." Nicky turned back to the demonic creature and saw that it was carrying a head under its arm, presumably its own. As Nicky watched, the head began to smile. A toothy grin spread across its face as its eyes glowed like embers, or an evil version of those dollar store glow sticks.

"That's really gross," Nicky whispered, as he started to back away from the figure. Will, however, had another plan. Standing up, he took his sword and held it high above his head with the blade toward the creature.

"Stand back," he said. Nicky didn't need to be told twice. He turned and began to run. Will yelled after him. "I said stand back, not run away!"

"I'm giving you room!" Nicky exclaimed as he attempted to run further, when suddenly his feet stopped moving and planted themselves on the ground. Unfortunately, the rest of his body flung off his feet, leaving two stumps where his feet used to be. He tumbled, footless, onto the lawn of an unsuspecting person and rolled onto his back to see Will squaring off the creature.

"Get back here, you coward!" Will called after him, and Nicky cursed. Picking small tufts of grass from his teeth, he crawled back to where his feet were and tried to reattach them.

"Come on feet. I can't run away from this beast if you're not attached!" He cried. Sadly, his feet didn't listen and seemed hesitant to re-join the rest of him. He turned back to Will and saw him slash at the creature with his sword. There was an incredible ease in the way Will fought. He moved with such grace and fluidity that it was hypnotic to watch. He was fast and moved so quickly it was hard to keep track of his whereabouts. Nicky could tell that he'd been well trained for this sort of interaction in the same way Nicky hadn't been.

Unfortunately, even though the demonic creature was large and bulky, it also appeared to know how to fight. It took its head and began to swing it on a chain as the horse attempted to flank Will. The head was screaming with laughter the entire time and Nicky contemplated on how such a feat, while visually terrifying, was a terrible battle tactic. Wouldn't they get dizzy swinging their head around like a morning star? Surely the creature hadn't thought itself through.

The beast swung its head and Will leapt back. Will took his sword and attempted to drive it through the creature's chest, but with a simple spin, the beast effortlessly evaded. Still on the grass, Nicky took his feet and tried to force them back on the bottom of his legs but they wouldn't connect.

"You need to get it back in the book!" Will called out.

"Is that going to be hard? That sounds like it'll be hard!"

"Point the book at it! Now!"

"Like a remote control?"

"I don't know what that is!" Will exclaimed. Nicky put down his feet and grabbed the book from his pack. He held it in his hand and pointed it at the creature. But nothing happened. He looked at the book and shook it a little in hopes that it would kick start something, but it did not. He knocked on it but still it did nothing. He held it up and pretended to fire it like it was a gun, but still nothing, even when he used the 'pew pew' sound effects.

"Do I open it?" he called out. Will ducked as the demon swung its head around and lobbed it at Will in a forceful launch. As it did, Will took his sword and jabbed it into the creature's side. This appeared to upset the beast, but didn't have much impact on it otherwise.

"Feel for the tab on the side and just point the book at it! Hit it!" The creature retreated for a moment and for the first time, seemed to notice Nicky. The horse bucked and jumped over Will, sending him flailing to the ground. Then, with a fury, the creature stormed towards Nicky.

With a yelp, Nicky clawed at the book. Doing the opposite of what Will had instructed him to do, he randomly opened the book in hopes that it would send the creature back to where it came from. Instead, when he opened it, he opened it backwards. Opening it towards himself, Nicky was instantly bathed in gallons of black ooze. The force was so strong that he was launched back with incredible force and the book landed on the lawn. The creature galloped away, not even bothering to trample Nicky further into the dirt.

Wiping giant globs of sludge from his eyes, Nicky watched as the book shot massive amounts of black energy into the world. Then, a massive swirling arm of energy burst from the pages, pulled itself out of the deluge, and let out a loud roar. Another arm followed and then a naked body emerged until a man the size of a house covered in black ooze ran screaming down the street. More of the ooze rained down as Nicky slowly crawled to the book. It took a lot of effort to get close, but when he did, the torrent of black energy was little more than a pathetic dribble spurting up from the pages like a peeing angel fountain. Using his hand, he closed it and laid on his back.

Looking up at the sky, soon Will looked down on him with a frown.

"I don't think I got it," he said. Will held up one of Nicky's disembodied feet and brought it down hard on his chest. Nicky recoiled as he debated for a second whether Will had just hit him or kicked him.

"You stupid! Stupid! Stupid!" He brought the foot down again, and again, until he had eased his temper. With one final thwack, he sat down in the sludgy goo next to Nicky and gave him his foot back. With a cough, Nicky sat up to join him.

"What was I supposed to do?"

"You were supposed to capture the demon and put it back into the compendium. Not release more of the demons inside. Especially not Oberon..."

"Was that what I was supposed to do?" Will bit his lip and gave Nicky back his other foot. "You weren't very good with instructions."

"What instructions exactly?" Nicky sassed. Will sighed and sat beside Nicky. Nicky couldn't help but notice that Will smelled like cinnamon. He definitely smelled better than the thick odour of ugly, oily sludge they were currently reclining in.

"I'll never be able to explain this, but here goes," Will began. "What you've done is... well, it's possibly the worst thing that's ever happened. The world is going to be plunged into chaos and darkness. The kingdoms will fall. The earth itself will tear apart. I don't want to overstate this—but we may all be royally and completely fucked."

"You think you got problems? I ruined my favourite shirt."

Nicky frowned at his shirt that now boldly declared 'WHITE POWER' to the world. Will shook his head.

"Next time, I should just let the demons kill you," Will said as he got up.

"Next time? You really think there's going to be a next time?"

"We don't have a choice. You just..."

"What the hell happened to my lawn?" a loud angry noise called out from behind them. Nicky had been so focused on what was going on he hadn't paid much attention to the yard that the battle had taken place in. What had started as a perfectly manicured plaza had quickly deteriorated into a jumble of dirt piles, torn flower beds, and a thick oily substance that resembled tar coating the ground like a glossy wrapping. When he turned around and saw the massive, angry black man carrying a shotgun, he knew that today would most likely continue to not be a great day.

"Sorry!" Nicky shrieked, and the two of them ran off. He wasn't sure where they were going, but if nothing else, he knew this—he would have to find a new shirt.

Chapter 5

The Chapter Where He Eats Cheesy Fries

Nicky lifted the fork full of cheese fries and stretched his jaw in a way that he normally reserved for greasy sandwiches. He may not be a warrior, but he could out-eat just about any-one.

"Your eating habits are appalling," Will grunted as he sat in the vinyl booth opposite Nicky. He had his arms crossed and had barely touched what could generously be described as a 'fast food.'

"You just have to learn how to unhinge your jaw. Then you can eat anything," Nicky replied between mouthfuls of the fatty, greasy meal. Just breathing it clogged up his arteries, but he didn't care. He would conquer these fries if it killed him. He'd had a hard day and deserved to treat himself.

"That is disturbing. Please put your mouth away. We need to discuss what this means." Will scratched his shoulder.

"Are you mad that man shot you?"

"That is upsetting, yes." Will cracked his jaw and stopped scratching at his wounded arm. Nicky didn't know why he was making such a big deal out of being shot. It had barely grazed him. "But if I'm going to be stuck with you, then you need to know some things."

"I'm not going to stop eating," Nicky replied, sending small pieces of fries propelling out into the air.

"Fine." Will pursed his lips and sat back in his chair. He peered out the window and quickly scoured the parking lot outside the diner. It was as if he was looking for something dangerous. "You've done something terrible."

"I work in a video store. I've done lots of terrible things. This one time, someone wanted to rent a video, but I hated them, so I put the wrong movie in their case." He picked up a small fry from the table and put it in his mouth. "On purpose." For a moment, Will was a statue before he remembered how to breathe.

"Somehow, every time you speak, I hate you more." Will gritted his teeth. "You have done something terrible. With this." Will pointed to the book. Nicky swallowed the fry. It lacked salt.

"You mean with the whole..."

"Yes," Will said. "I mean with the whole thing. Everything. Every choice that you have made since acquiring this book is worse than the last. Every time you get the chance to redeem yourself, you have blown it. You are either the stupidest man I have ever met, or just so incredibly unobservant that it's a miracle you haven't died from walking off a bridge."

"Bridges have guard rails. They're surprisingly hard to walk off of." Will slammed his hands down on the table so hard that the table buckled. Nicky pointed at the table. "That's not a very nice thing to do to a table."

"Stop. Whatever it is you think you're doing, stop. I just need you to shut up and listen to the words that I am telling you right now with your ears, so, just shut up, and listen to the... listen."

"That wasn't a very good..."

"It got away from me!" he bellowed. Several other patrons

of the diner turned to them and shushed. Will reached across the table, grabbed Nicky by the collar, and pulled him close. So close he could smell him. Again, he smelled like cinnamon, which made Nicky hungry. "You're meddling in supernatural affairs, okay? You're in the middle of a paranormal battle between humans and non-humans and if you're not careful, not only will you die, but every living thing on this planet will suffer. Do you understand that?"

"That sounds bad," Nicky said as he looked deep into Will's crystal blue eyes. "You sure?"

"Yes." Will held the 's' for an uncomfortable amount of time. "Yes, I am sure." Nicky wasn't convinced.

"Can you prove it?" Will's face twitched, and he slowly sat back in his chair. He looked so infuriated that Nicky wondered if smoke would start to pour out of his nose.

"Your hands and your legs have unattached and reattached themselves and yet here you are again, fully corporeal. How do you explain that?"

"Maybe I just had leprosy. You don't know these things." Nicky crossed his arms and leaned back in the vinyl chair, making it squeak. Will clenched his fork so tightly it bent.

"It doesn't work like that. Your body is coursing with fae energy and, as a result, there are things that are going to want to stop you. Things that are going to want to kill you."

"Well, why should I believe you?"

"Because I'm a fae, you nitwit!" Nicky paused when he looked at Will.

"What now?"

"A fae. A fairy you twit!" Nicky sat back and considered Will again. Sure, he was well dressed, but this news still came as quite a shock. He'd never met a fairy before.

"Well, good for you. I try not to judge. I mean I would consider myself more on the pan level but don't worry. I won't judge you. I'll have you know I once watched a movie with a gay in it. I didn't like it much, but I did it anyway!"

"Not like that. I mean like magic! Power. A force," Will snapped at him. Nicky contemplated this for a moment.

"Like the force? In that space movie?"

"I don't know what you're talking about, but yes. Yes. Whatever you say it is, it's like that. And this little book that you have now is, or should I say was, a prison for some of the most bad fae of the world. It has been used by the high court for hundreds of years to imprison the faefolk and creatures that seek to kill, destroy and cause other chaos out there. And now the book is empty, and you have unleashed hundreds of evil, destructive creatures into a world that is woefully unprepared for them. So if we don't find a way to get them back, hundreds, thousands, maybe even millions of people will die. Is that what you want?"

Nicky's eyes went wide with fear.

"Oh no! We have to go!" Nicky said. Will clapped his hands as the two of them sprung to their feet. Will threw down a bill and chased Nicky as he raced outside.

"Perfect! I didn't think you'd jump into this so enthusiastically, but colour me pleased! Come on, we've got to go to the forest to..." Will paused as Nicky turned away from him and began to run deeper into the city. Confused, Will jogged over to him and stopped him. "What are you doing? The forest is that way."

"Hey, if you want to go cruising, that's your business. I've got somewhere I have to go," Nicky uttered as he side stepped Will and trotted away. Will once again ran in front of him and grabbed Nicky, freezing him in place.

"Did you hear nothing I just said? There's a massive evil force coming and..."

"I know! That's why I have to get there before Seven!" Will blinked at him in response.

"What?"

Chapter 6

The Chapter Where Mom Drinks

To some people, Nicky's mom could be described as a little much. To others, she was a lot much. Tonight, she was wearing zebra skin tights that hugged her hips so hard it was a miracle no one had called animal control. Her vibrant red hair looked more like a mane than a hairstyle. Her make up was caked on so thick you could eat it with a spoon. She sat in front of the meal she had made, beaming with pride as Nicky and Will sat with half consumed plates. Nicky looked relatively relaxed. Will appeared to be so tense he could turn coal into a diamond.

In front of them was a smorgasbord of spam, potatoes, bacon, more spam and fried greens that smelled like a convenience store explosion.

Will crossed his arms. Sitting opposite of Nicky, he tried to appear pleasant but couldn't hide his distaste for the situation. There were bigger and more life-threatening concerns to be handled right now, but he was currently stuck here and couldn't get Nicky to budge. All Nicky seemed concerned about was his mother's boyfriend.

"Hey Bill! Bill baby, bring the soda. I think Nicky's friend is thirsty." She turned to Will and placed one of her long fingers on his shoulder. Her nails were almost as long as the rest of her hand. They smelled like gasoline and allspice. "You should have a drink, dear. I can get you something stronger if you like."

"I am fine. Thank you for your hospitality," Will said, trying to be polite, but his patience was wearing thin. His meal was nearly untouched.

"Bill! Bring me some whisky! It's for his little friend." She turned to Nicky and put her hand on his shoulder. "Nicky baby, tell mama what's going on with you. Are you enjoying the store?"

"It's okay."

"My friend Martha went there, you know. She said she saw you. She said that she went home and someone had forgotten to rewind the video. Was that you, Nicky?"

"It wasn't me, mom." Nicky shifted uncomfortably and Will glared at him. If the room was quiet, everyone could've heard the sound of Will's teeth grinding. Luckily, his mother never stopped talking long enough for that to be a concern.

"I knew it. I knew it wouldn't have been you. Not my baby, I told her. Not mine!" She ruffled his hair and smiled at him. "I knew it. So tell me, who is your little friend?"

"He's not my... look, he's a fairy, alright?"

"I mean, I'm technically a fae but..." Will began, but was interrupted by a squeal of delight.

"Oh! My god! You have a fairy friend! That's so progressive!" She turned to Will with a smile that stretched beyond the capabilities of nature. Beaming at him, Will noticed a healthy smattering of lipstick coating her teeth. "Good for you, dear. You're just being you! That's so good of you! You know my hairdresser is a fairy. He's a beautiful one too! I went there last time and just had to tell myself that it was such a shame that someone as cute as him would go to waste. I can give you his number. I think he's single."

"I'm not that kind of..."

"Hold on. Let me get his number. Okay? Okay, love. I'll be right back. Bill! BILL! We got one in the house!" she bellowed as she staggered her way into the kitchen. Finally alone, Will turned his attention to Nicky and frowned.

"Your mother enjoys her alcohol."

"Wine. She loves wine," Nicky said. "Might even love it more than me."

"She is excessively fond of it. And I assure you, I also would prefer wine to you. And I hate wine." Will took a moment to examine the house. "You shouldn't have come here. It's not safe."

"No kidding. She didn't even make a dessert," Nicky said as he scooped up a ladle full of slop and let it drip back into the stew-like meal. "This meatloaf is terrible."

"No. By coming here, you have put her and potentially her friend Bill in great danger."

"Bill isn't her friend. He's her lover. It's disgusting, isn't it?"

"I don't feel it's my place to judge these affairs," Will said as he picked up his fork. A large clump of spam hung to the end of it. He put it back down slowly, as if it would spring to life at any moment.

"I guess a fairy would say that," Nicky said as he sat back in his chair. He exhaled as he looked around the dining room. "I used to live here, you know."

"I presumed as much."

"It doesn't smell as nice." Nicky sneered as he looked around.

"It smelled nicer before he was here all the time."

"You don't seem to like this Bill person much."

"Because he's an asshole," Nicky said. "I really don't think..."

Suddenly, a rock flew through the window, showering Nicky and Will in a hail of broken glass. Startled, Nicky staggered out of his chair and landed on his back. Will gripped his sword and swung it towards the window, preparing to strike. When Nicky landed, the wind freshly knocked out of him, he watched the rock collide with his mother's hutch, sending pieces of commemorative plates flying throughout the room. Then, the rock stood up and looked at him before flipping him off.

"It's a thing!" Nicky yelled. The rock looked at him, or now that it was still, he could tell it was something more akin to a small goblin than a rock. Two thin legs and arms sprung out as a pair of beady black eyes turned towards Nicky with a bloodthirsty rage. A bloody smile spread across its impish face as it lunged at him, opening his mouth wide to reveal rows and rows of sharp teeth in its oversized mouth. Nicky screamed in defence, but shockingly, it did nothing. Will ran to his side and scooped up the creature with the blunt side of his sword and launched it into the air. He then swung his sword back and thwacked it like a bat, sending the small creature screaming into the outside world.

"Move," Will said. Nicky scrambled to his feet and made his way into the TV room. He was about to turn and go into the kitchen when Will stopped him.

"My mom..."

"Is in danger. If you go to her, they'll attack her. If we leave, they'll follow us. Come on."

"But we're Italian! If we don't say goodbye, she'll kill us!" Will

43

grabbed him and pushed him towards the door. Putting their shoes on, they could hear the sound of small nails scratching against the wood. Will was the first to exit and they could see a small swarm of the tiny creatures gathering around outside. Will punted one of them against a tree. It collided with a thud and then burst into ashes.

Another one leapt at them from the roof of the house, carrying in its teeth a shingle from the roof. Will smacked that one, causing it to collide with the ground and severing its own head with the shingle before bursting into dust. Moving gracefully, Will ushered Nicky across the yard to the street. He was walking quickly and Nicky found himself having to jog just to keep up, which he had always hated.

"Not very effective killers, are they?"

"Maybe not, but they're tenacious, and they're going to follow us," Will said as they raced down the cul-de-sac.

"Why?"

"Because they want to kill you so they can take possession of that book. And we can't let that happen."

"Why not? I don't want it anymore," Nicky grumbled.

"They're clearly being controlled, and I suspect I know by who. This person is after the book because if they get it, then we can't seal them away again. And civilization, as you know it, will be destroyed."

"Right. And that would be bad, right?" Will kept walking. "Okay, okay, just stop for a second." Will did. He turned to Nicky with contempt radiating off of him.

"What?"

"What were those things?"

"Gremlins. Red Caps to be exact. Little goblins that want to kill you and then use your blood to dye their hats."

"That's disgusting." Nicky looked back at the house and felt a pang of guilt. "Mom's okay, right?"

"She'll be fine as long as we don't go back," Will said. "But that's not my biggest concern right now. It's getting dark. We need to find a place to stay for the night."

"Well. I think I know a place we could stay if you're up for it."

"I don't have a choice, do I?" Will asked, but Nicky was already racing down the street as fast as his clumsy feet would take him.

Chapter 7

THE CHAPTER WHERE THEY FIGHT AND STUFF

"What do you call this place?" Will asked as he followed Nicky through the dark entranceway. Nicky turned to him, beaming with pride.

"Mideo Video. It's kind of like my home away from home. I'm here fifteen hours a week! Sometimes even sixteen," he said as they walked in. "Here, let me turn on the lights..."

"Don't. We don't want to let anyone know we're here," Will said. He looked around and even in the darkness, Nicky could tell he was frowning. There was a smell thick in the air that smelled like stale popcorn, burning plastic and farts. To Nicky, it smelled like home. "Why did you think this place would be a good hiding space?"

"Look around. There are no windows. Only one exit. It's crowded enough to make people slightly claustrophobic, but not crowded enough for people to feel creeped out by that. Clear sightlines from everywhere to the front door. I figured it would come in handy." Will looked around as if to confirm everything that Nicky was saying. This was indeed a concrete death trap. It would do. Contented, he looked at Nicky with a nod.

"It will suffice. Good thinking." Nicky felt almost proud when

Will said that. Maybe he was winning him over. He likely wasn't, but maybe.

"Cool. I'll make some popcorn," Nicky said as he sauntered to the popcorn machine, but Will quickly stepped into his path. Nicky looked up and down and shot his gaze between the popcorn machine and the stern face of Will. "Will, I can't make popcorn if you're blocking my path."

"We have more important things to do than eat popcorn," he said as he unsheathed his sword and pointed it directly at Nicky. "Face me."

"I am facing you."

"No. Draw your weapon."

"I don't have a pen?"

"What?"

"How can I draw a weapon without a pen?" Will clenched his jaw and squeezed his sword.

"Just... look, you need to learn how to fight. I'm here to teach you how."

"Why now?" Nicky whined. "I'm tired."

"Because it needs to be done. And now is as good a time as any. So come on. Fight me."

"But I don't want to fight. Look, I'm already breaking the rules by letting us in here after hours. Isn't that enough rebellion for one day?" Nicky droned.

"Do you want to be ready for the attacks that are going to be coming your way, or would you rather just roll over and die?" Nicky stepped around Will and made his way to the machine. He considered the question.

"Is dying an option?"

"I'm trying to help." Will gritted his teeth.

"And I'm trying to unwind after a long, hard day. What part of that don't you understand?" Frustrated, Will grunted and swung the sword. Nicky ducked, causing Will to smash his weapon into a collection of Terminatrix VHS tapes. A few magnetic tapes burst out and un-spooled across the floor.

"This is for your own good! You're not going to last if you're not prepared!" Will yelled as he swung at Nicky again, this time lodging his sword in the crotch of an oversized corporate cartoon mouse standee.

"Then I'll enjoy what I can now!" Nicky retorted. Will swung, and Nicky blocked it with a copy of 'The Three Musketeers'. "You're going to damage the tapes!"

"Not my concern," he said as he calmly backed Nicky into a corner. "I'm here to ensure you don't die."

"By killing me?" Nicky put up his hands in a fighting stance. He didn't know which one it was, but he'd seen it in a movie once. "Watch out. I know Sudoku!"

"I somehow doubt that." Will took the sword and wedged it under a tape and flicked it in the air. Launching it in the air, he held the sword back like a baseball bat and swung. It smashed directly into the tape and sent it flying, crashing into the wall beside Nicky. It burst open and Nicky ran over to catch the pieces before it shattered on the ground. "Hey! That's a classic! If you're going to kill me, then kill me, but keep the movies out of it!"

"I'm not going to kill you. I'm trying to..." Will began, but Nicky acted quickly. Taking the movie, he slammed it into Will's head with a distinctive clunk. Will collapsed and Nicky threw himself behind the checkout counter. Like a brave lemming, he cowered underneath it, expecting Will to get up and come to kill him any moment. Gripping onto a fire extinguisher, he waited for Will to appear, but he never did. After a minute of nothing, he peeked over the counter to see Will still laying down. He slowly got up and peered over at him. Was he broken?

"Will?" he whispered when the phone rang. He wasn't sure what instinct made him answer it, but he brought the receiver to his ear and responded in a chipper tone.

"Mideo Video. Your most adequate movie spot."

"Hi. Are you guys open late? Like really late?" a female voice asked.

"No. It's really late. So we're actually closed."

"But you're there," she cooed. She sounded sweet. Her voice buzzed with energy. It sent shivers shooting through his body and he felt self-conscious talking to her. Could she tell he was nervous? Did she even care? Was he blowing it? "Can I come too?" She emphasised the verb.

"You want a video?" he gulped. He could feel himself sweating. He never sweated on the phone before. He began to wonder if she was hot. Then he wondered if that was sexist. Then he wondered if he cared.

"I want someone to talk to. I guess I could use a movie. Would you like to show me one?"

"I'll show you anything," he giggled. He could feel himself getting hot and bothered. There was something in her voice that sounded so warm and inviting. He had to find out who this woman was. He had already suspected that he was in love with her, whatever love was.

"I want you to show me something, then. Where would you want me?"

"Oh. Okay. Well, why not come by? I'll be here."

"Ten minutes. Don't keep me waiting." The phone clicked and Nicky couldn't help but grin. She was coming here! The mystery woman with the sexy voice was coming here! She would see him in his natural environment! While he couldn't be entirely sure, he was positive he'd seen a porno once about a video rental store. Maybe this was his chance to live out his deepest, darkest fantasy of being the manager.

He looked over the store and realised he had a big problem. Will was still laying in the middle of the aisle. He rushed over to him and sat on top of him. He grabbed his face and tapped him a few times.

"Will? Will, are you in there? Look buddy, I kind of need this space," he urged, but Will didn't respond. He was out. For a moment he assumed Will to be dead, but then realised he was still breathing when he held his hand to his mouth. On the one hand, he was thankful that he wasn't a murderer, but on the other, seeing an unconscious man on the ground of his store would likely be a mood killer for the mystery woman. "I'm going to move you, okay? It's not a bad thing. It's just so I can get laid. Maybe. If she's up for it," he said. "I know you'd understand if you weren't... you know. Okay, good talk."

He grabbed the mop bucket and managed to shuffle Will into it. He probably should have dumped all the water out, but he didn't have time. Will would understand.

While the store was big enough to hold dozens of movies, it didn't have a lot of empty space to hold unconscious cockblockers. He assumed that if things went well that he'd be using the back room, meaning that he'd have to store Will in either the bathroom or the broom closet. Thinking it would be the easier of the two, he wheeled Will over to the broom closet and managed to stuff him inside between the mop and the collection of almost never used dusters. Just in time, too. As soon as he had successfully sequestered him, there was a knock on the door and Nicky ran to answer it.

If she had sounded sexy on the phone, nothing could have prepared him for her beauty in person. She was stunning. Her eyes were beautifully framed by a bright pink eyeshadow that matched her cheeks. Her lips were painted blue, which matched her eyes. Her dark hair was up in a side ponytail that had streaks of blonde coursing through it. She almost looked like a real woman, but he was about to spend time with her, so she must've been an angel. Nicky flipped the lock and opened the door for her to come in.

"Thank you," she purred as she sauntered in. "Nice place you got here. Lots of space."

"Yeah," he said. Then he started to laugh. It was a very uncomfortable laugh and the more he tried to suppress it, the more violent the laugh became. After what felt like an eternity, he finally got it under control. She smiled at him with her eyes and frowned with her pouty mouth. "Sorry. I don't know what that was."

"Are you nervous or something? You shouldn't be. You already got me in here. What's a girl to do?" She walked towards him and didn't stop until she had him cornered against the counter. He laughed again.

"You're..." His voice stopped making words. She just smiled at him.

"You talk too much." She kissed him. Her mouth tasted like cigarettes and bubble gum. Her tongue was agile, penetrating sections of his mouth that had never been kissed before. Her body firmly pressed into his as she pinned him down. She was aggressive. Much more so than he had expected.

"You know what you're doing."

"Don't worry. I'll take it easy on you," she said with a laugh. For a moment, Nicky laughed as well. It was good. For a moment, he was happy.

Then her face transformed into a hideous fish monster.

Chapter 8

THE CHAPTER WHERE HE MAKES OUT WITH A FISH MONSTER

Most people would probably stop making out with someone once they had transformed into a hideous fish monster. But Nicky was not like most people. For one, he tried to be open-minded about these things. Maybe it was a skin condition. Or maybe she was a nice hideous fish monster. It wasn't his place to judge. Either way, she was an amazing kisser, and it had been a long time since he'd been with a woman, so he couldn't afford to be picky now.

They moved into the back room, which was little more than a glorified storage area with a table that had three automatic rewind machines proudly displayed on it. There was a mini fridge where he kept his food and then forgot about it for months on end, and a couch where unspeakable horrors occurred regularly. Now, it looked like one more such occurrence would be happening.

Nicky didn't kiss well, but he liked to think that he kissed with extreme enthusiasm and joie de vivre. What he lacked in experience, he made up for in waggling and creativity. In his head, he began to cycle through all the various kissing techniques he had invented. Some of his favourites were the tongue darter, the monster masher and the flick and spit. She didn't seem to enjoy the last one, but the other two proved adequate.

The space was limited, but Nicky didn't care. As their kissing intensified, her macking technique became rougher. Her sharp pointy teeth began to slice at his tongue, but he was sure he could create new techniques to counteract that. Soon, he began darting his tongue in and out at a rapid pace as she tried to chew at it. It almost became like a game until she finally growled and pinned him down.

"Stop that," she growled.

"Stop what?"

"That tongue thing. Stop it."

"I thought you liked it."

"Just stop," she said before opening her mouth and bringing it down on his neck.

"What's wrong with it?" he asked, but she didn't stop chewing on his neck. "Seriously? What was wrong with it?" With a frustrated sigh, she sat up and looked at him with her weird fish eyes.

"It just doesn't work for me. Okay? Now, can you just let me finish eating your neck?" She went back to try to continue chewing on his neck, but he sat her beside him instead. She blinked at him. "What?"

"Can you at least give me tips?"

"Later. Okay?" She once again tried to clamp onto his neck, but he pushed her off and stood over her.

"Look, I'm all for feminism and for women taking control of a situation. I didn't even care when you turned into a fish lady, but right now you're taking advantage of my generosity, and I don't appreciate it. Now, it's not that I don't appreciate getting a hickey with teeth, if that's your thing, fine... but don't critique my technique and then blow me off."

Then she roared. Nicky didn't even realise that a fish woman could roar, but here she was doing it like a boss. It sounded like an angry whale that had just stepped on Lego. Then she lunged at him, grabbing his hand, and caused it to separate from the rest of him.

"Dammit. Do you know how hard that is to put back on?" he grunted. She lunged at him again, and he fumbled back. Then he got the sense he might be in trouble.

With no speed and less grace, he lunged towards the door and she leapt after him. He simply stepped out of the way, causing her to tumble into a pile of VHS cases. They tumbled over her and Nicky, thinking as fast as he was able to, sauntered to the door. He ran into the main area of the store and shut the door behind him. He looked around the dark store and there was a tapping sound coming from the janitorial closet.

He walked over and opened the door to see a very wet and very angry Will glaring at him.

"What's up?" Nicky asked.

"I'm wet."

"Hi wet. I'm Nicky." Will grit his teeth and attempted to suppress the anger that clearly wanted to bubble out of him. In an angry motion, Will brushed past him and, without saying a word, went to the door of the backroom. "You might not want to go in there?" Will turned to him with a sour expression.

"And why not?" Suddenly, there was a roar and claws scratching at the door. Will glared at Nicky. "What did you do?"

"She wanted a movie. And then she kissed me," Nicky responded. "Hand to God that's all that happened."

"Your neck is bleeding."

"That's where she kissed me. I just don't think she's very good at it. Normally, the bleeding stops by now." Will exhaled.

"Wait here." Will grabbed his sword. He sounded tired and irritated. Nicky suspected he was both. Will took the doorknob in his hand, turned it, and slammed his shoulder into the door. The door burst open and the fish monster erupted past him. She pushed Will into the wall with a solid clunk and flung herself over the counter as she closed in on Nicky. Nicky, being a brave man, ran.

The fish woman skidded past him. She collided hard with the shelving unit that contained a wealth of British romantic comedies. The shelf toppled over, crashing into the musical section, which then crashed into children's movies. Soon most of the movie shelves were toppled, leaving the floor covered in rogue tapes and cases. He quietly hoped he wouldn't need to be the one to clean this all up. Maybe he'd get lucky and die instead.

"What do I do?" Nicky hollered. He looked towards Will when the fish woman leapt between them. Her long, pink fingernails were sharp and looked more like small daggers. She growled at him, revealing rows of shiny teeth that glowed in the fluorescent lights. She was about to lunge at him when Will came by and used the blunt side of his sword to pull her away. She struggled, but Will pressed himself close to her as he struggled to get her to stop coming after Nicky.

"Use the book!" Will called out. He grabbed the book and threw it with his free hand, causing the book to collide with Nicky's face. Nicky sneezed in indignation.

"You jerk! That really hurt!"

"Just use the damn book!" Will screamed as the creature

roared again. It sounded a lot less threatening when the air was being choked out of her. Almost like a vibrating gargle.

"Fine! I'll use it then. Stupid jerk," he muttered as he lifted the book.

"Just warn me before you...-" Will began, but Nicky didn't wait and opened the book. At least he opened it the right way this time. As he did, the creature screamed out once and began to glow. Soon, a burst of black energy shot from her and she transformed into a blast of ink. Like the last bit of milkshake through a straw, she was sucked into the book as it closed.

The store was quiet and Nicky let out a small chuckle of victory.

Nicky felt victorious! He lifted the book up and laughed. "I did it! I did a thing! It worked!" He looked up excitedly, only to realise he was now alone. He looked at the space where Will had been and found that they had both vanished. He looked from the empty space, to the book, and back to the empty space.

"Whoops."

Suddenly, there was a sound more terrifying than any Nicky could've prepared himself for. He looked at the clock and cursed as he marvelled at the destruction of the store. The only person who could be coming into the store at this hour would be the only person he truly feared. He was about to confront... his boss.

Chapter 9

THE CHAPTER WHERE HE'S CAUGHT

Nicky realized that standing in the middle of his work, in the middle of the night, wearing a *WHITE POWER* t-shirt, covered in blood, surrounded by dozens of damaged videos and empty cases—was probably not a good look. That being said, he was like a deer in headlights. He wanted to move, but he couldn't. His feet were planted to the ground, and he was getting nervous, which was not an emotion he normally felt.

His boss shuffled into the store, looking more grumpy than anything else. He looked around, seemingly unphased by the massive amount of damage to his merchandise, but froze when he saw Nicky.

"What are you doing here?" he asked. He was a big man who constantly sounded like he was chewing tobacco, even when he wasn't. Maybe his tongue was too big for his mouth. He wore a name tag that said "Vincent" but wanted people to call him Vinnie. Nicky called him Vinny, just to be different.

"I wanted a movie?" Nicky replied.

"Okay," Vinny said. He motioned to the knocked over shelves and the tapes on the ground. "You do that?"

"No," he lied. "Earthquake?"

"Happens," Vinny said. "Wanna grab a beer?"

"Here?"

"Why not?"

"I can't argue that logic." Nicky shrugged his compliance and followed Vinny into the back room. Over time they'd become friends, creating codes and in jokes that only they knew. It was nice to have someone to talk about movies with—even if they didn't always have much else to talk about.

Vinny froze in the middle of the trashed space and sniffed with a grimace. "Smells like fish."

"Does it? I had no idea," Nicky said. Vinny looked at him and eyed him with a greasy smirk.

"Good for you," he said, smacking Nicky on his bleeding neck. "Didn't think you'd have it in you, but looks like it was rough. Got you good on the neck there."

"What?" Nicky asked, as Vinny slung himself onto the sofa. He then reached up to an old children's film and opened it, revealing a warm can of beer. He grabbed another one and tossed it to Nicky, then tapped the couch beside him. Nicky sat beside him, a bit unsure of what was happening. "I always wondered why you had Betamax here."

"We're in a glorious business here. Ladies love videos. Most of 'em would kill to be in one. Drives them nuts. You like a nutty woman, don't ya?"

"I mean, I don't really focus on flavours," Nicky said.

"It's all about them chicks who go crazy for movies. If you promise them a free rental, a lot of them will do just about anything. One time, a girl flashed me her bra strap. It's glorious," he sighed, as he suckled from his beer can as foam spurted across him. "The other half doesn't see it the way I do."

"Did she kick you out again?" Nicky asked. He was always

surprised that Vinny was married. He had met his wife twice and both times she didn't seem to enjoy it there. In fact, she didn't seem to enjoy it much. But knowing Vinny, that didn't surprise him.

Vinny nodded as he took a long sip of his beer.

"She thinks I'm philandering. I told her I didn't understand her word choice, so she kicked me out." Nicky put his beer down and looked at Vinny. "She said I was a philanderer."

"I can't imagine why. Isn't that where you give your money to a good cause?"

"Makes sense. She hates being nice." Vinny laid back on the couch and looked at Nicky strangely. "Didn't you used to have two hands?"

Nicky looked down. He had completely forgotten that the fish lady had taken his hand. He quickly looked around the back room and wondered where she could have dropped it. Then he felt a moderate ping of dread as he realised it was very likely that she still had it when he had made the book eat her.

Damn. He was going to miss that hand.

"Yeah. Should be around here somewhere," he said, trying to sound casual.

"Yeah. Alright. That makes sense." Vinny said through a massive yawn. "I'm just going to shut my eyes for a minute. You good?"

"I mean..." Before he could even respond, Vinny was out.

Nicky had never seen anyone fall asleep so quickly. The beer was still resting on his belly. Miraculously, the beer didn't spill a drop. It gave the impression he had done this move many times before.

Despite his boss passing out, Nicky was still restless. Not just because there was a burly man taking up most of the couch space and he wasn't sure how to properly cuddle him consensually, but because he found himself at a loss of what to do next. Once the snoring started, he knew he'd have to get out of the room, so he did the only thing he knew he could do and decided to go on a hunt for his wandering hand.

Luckily, it didn't take him long to find. It was clutching a copy of the Addams family and was pried on to it pretty good. Using his still attached hand as a wrench, he did manage to get it free, but it wasn't reattaching to his wrist. Improvising, he used some duct tape and rolled it on so that his hand at least looked like it was mostly attached. It wasn't pretty, but it wasn't his dominant hand, so he didn't need to worry. Not yet, at least. With that done, he did the only thing left and went out onto the store floor and began to clean.

He put the shelves back. He put the movies back one by one until all of them were off the floor. He found some that needed to be repaired and put them aside. He had expected this job to take hours, but once everything was complete, it had been barely a half hour. He wondered if work would always be this quick if he didn't slack off so often, but then brushed it off as a fluke.

He sat in the children's section and sighed as he looked at the covers of the movies when suddenly he noticed a movie he had never seen before. It was a plain case which he'd never noticed- but it was covered with writing all over it. Phrases like *Don't watch this video, Deadly essence inside! Do not open* and *Danger! Destroy this tape!* covered the front and the back of it. He smiled as he held it close and knew exactly what to do with it.

He was going to watch it.

Chapter 10

THE CHAPTER WHERE HE WATCHED A TAPE

While he couldn't be sure that what he was about to watch was porn, Nicky felt certain that it was. Mideo Video had been unique in the sense that they didn't offer much in the way of traditional pornography, but this video proved that they might've- so maybe they could again someday.

With a sense of awe and wonder, Nicky placed the movie in the VCR behind the counter and hunkered down on the floor. With a bowl of stale popcorn and a large bottle of fizzy sugar water, he clicked play. As it hummed into life, he cheered as the screen sputtered to life. To his disappointment, a man appeared; not that this man was anything but strapping, but it was definitely not what he had been expecting. Normally these things started with a classroom, or a pirate ship, or a dingy bedroom, and this man seemed to be in none of these places. Sure, he was attractive enough, but there was something strangely familiar about him. Maybe he'd already seen this one, or more likely, the man just got around.

"So you're the fool who set me free?" the man onscreen asked, to no one in particular. Nicky took the moment to examine him. He was thick with muscle and had hair like a wild man. His eyes were hypnotising and seemed to spiral around themselves. He was undoubtedly handsome and Nicky leaned back- perhaps this wouldn't be a waste after all. He took his free hand and rested it against his stomach—just in case.

Unhinging his jaw to allow for maximum ability, Nicky took a large mouthful of popcorn. It was stale but salty and he'd certainly had worse. For a moment he lost himself, before looking up and seeing that the movie hadn't seemed to progress at all. The man onscreen looked directly out, seemingly at him. Nicky took a moment to examine the man's eyes more fully and smiled.

"Are you the one who opened the book?" The man seemed to want an answer, but from whom? There didn't seem to be anyone else in the movie. "Can you even hear me? You're not reacting much to what I'm saying here." Nicky squinted at the man.

"Me?" Nicky asked.

"Are you the fool who set me free?" The man looked expectant. Nicky frowned. "If you can understand what I'm saying, just say..."

"Great, all those warnings for a kids flick," he muttered, and the man on screen seemed to get even more irritated.

"You there! Sitting on the floor!" Nicky looked at the handsome man and paused. Was he actually talking to a screen?

"Me?"

"Yes you! Who else would I be speaking with?" the man spat. Nicky shrugged.

"I don't know your life. I thought you were a movie. You didn't respond before. Dialogue is a two-way street."

"A supernatural being is speaking to you from a magical device. Shouldn't that be enough?" the man uttered. Nicky shrugged, but deeper this time.

"It's not magical- it's a VCR. We just run it through the wire so that we don't have to..." The man waved his hand and Nicky stopped speaking. It looked like he was getting frustrated- but Nicky wasn't sure why.

"I can see magic doesn't impress you. I need your assistance. You shall meet me for a drink. Take me to where you have your finest mead and we shall discuss the terms of your surrender." Nicky pointed to himself.

"You want to meet with me?" Nicky asked.

"We must. It is urgent, and you are the one who released me." Nicky scratched his head.

"Is this... a date?"

"Just find me a place with mead and we shall discuss!"

"I don't even know who you are? What are we..."

"Tomorrow. When the sun is its highest." Nicky blinked at him. The man shook his head. "Noon. Meet me at noon."

"Do I have-"

"Yes. You must. It is imperative. Tomorrow at noon. Do not be late."

"Okay. Fine. Whatever... but can I choose the place?"

Chapter 11

THE CHAPTER WITH THE ANIMATRONIC HAWK

Some would call Nicky's choice in the venue immature. Many would, in fact. Actually, to be more specific—all would. Deep down, even he knew it was, but he couldn't help it. When it came to animatronic wonder and the smell of cheap pizza, no one could top Pizza Hawk's Rock-n-Roll Pizzeria and Pizza Palace.

There was something about this place that reminded him of home. Maybe it was the smell of grease and desperation- or maybe it was just the fact that it was dark, messy, cramped and also smelled like grease and desperation. Whatever it was, he felt comfortable- like he belonged.

He'd picked out his favourite seats as well. Sitting in the centre of the dank restaurant provided him a great view of the stage, the arcade, and most importantly Pizza Hawk. Every half hour the seven foot tall animatronic monstrosity that had neglected to age gracefully years ago would come out and play a set of dated songs with lyrics changed to pizza puns. While he waited, he scoped out the space and ensured he knew where everything was. Marking the exits, he also made a note of a kid's birthday party he could use as human shields to protect himself if he needed to.

He took a bite of his rubbery pizza, which tasted less like

plastic than last week, but more like plastic than the week before that, before turning his attention to his flat root beer. One thing he enjoyed about this place was the bottomless drinks. He was one of the few adults who could spend any amount of time in here without resorting to something alcoholic.

After a rousing edition of *Slice Slice Baby*, the man from the porno appeared in the doorway. He took up most of it despite the fact that it was a set of double doors. His massive head brushed the ceiling and his shoulders barely squeezed through. He must've been eight feet tall hunched over and when he stood, he had to tilt his head to not bash it on the ceiling. Nicky waved at him and somehow, with great effort, the brute manoeuvred his way to the table and sat.

"You brought the book?" he asked. His voice was low and gruff. He sounded angry. Judging by his angry expression, Nicky guessed that he most likely was.

"It's impolite to join someone at a table and not introduce yourself." The man's face looked rougher in person. Like it had survived a battle with a blender and then went to a back alley for discount plastic surgery. His beard was full and bushy, and his hair was tied back with a green scrunchy. His clothes looked like they had been painted on and displayed his rippling physique, leaving nothing to the imagination. Despite this, he still was an aggressively attractive man, albeit one who had been left in a growth chamber too long.

"You have no need to call me anything."

"I'm not going to let you sit with me if I don't even know your name." Nicky looked at the large man defiantly. If he thought things through, the man could have crushed his head without breaking a sweat. Luckily for him, the large man extended his hand.

"Call me Oberon, if you must."

"Nicky. Nice to meet you, Oberon. That a French name?" he asked, offering his hand to Oberon. Who then took it. Nicky looked down and realised that his still unattached hand was once again lost, and Oberon seemed to be doing a thumb war with it. He cursed the duct tape under his breath. Now he'd have to find another way to reattach it. "Sorry."

Oberon didn't offer it back. Instead, he put it down beside the pizza and leaned back in his chair, which was comically small for his gargantuan size. Realising he would not be able to balance on only one chair, he grabbed another and rested himself between them. Even with the extra support, his legs couldn't fit under the table so he was forced to straddle it in a way that made Nicky question whether it was sexual or not. Oberon crossed his arms and looked down at Nicky.

"I do not like it here. The music is unpleasant."

"The first dozen times you hear it, it's awful. But then it becomes better. You might even enjoy it. I ordered for us. If you want a slice, dig in." Oberon reached down and grabbed half of the pizza between his fingers. He sniffed it and Nicky wondered if he was checking for poison. Then he wondered why he hadn't thought to poison it. Then he remembered that he'd put pineapple on it, and that maybe that would be enough. With a flick, Oberon flung the pie into his mouth and devoured it in one gulp. Nicky waited several seconds, but to his dismay, Oberon didn't die. Maybe next time he'd try adding olives.

"You! Wench! Grab me a mead!" Oberon bellowed to a young woman wearing a yellow fox head cap and tail. The woman looked at him for a second before rolling her eyes and disappearing into the kitchen. He turned back to Nicky. "She heard me, right?"

"Everyone heard you. So yes." Nicky said. He gave a quick glance around the room, seeing that the majority of the patrons had turned to see what the commotion was about.

"Return your gaze to the Hawk god!" Oberon yelled as he motioned his massive hand to Pizza Hawk. Everyone instantly snapped back to their meals, and Oberon twitched. "I require mead. Will she get it for me?"

"She'll be back. She's probably busy." Nicky said as he reached across the table and tried to fit his hand back onto his wrist stump. It still wouldn't reattach. "I don't suppose you could help me out with this?"

"No. I will destroy you. But enough of the formalities..." Oberon scratched at his beard with a frown. "Where is the book?"

"I've got it. I just didn't bring it with me."

"What?!" Oberon yelled. He stood up so fast that it flung his head straight into the ceiling. Plaster and dust fell down as everyone turned to gawk again. One woman shrieked, but Nicky was unsure whether it was a customer, a patron, or someone from the apartment upstairs. Bringing his head back down into the space Oberon reached across the table, grabbed Nicky's neck and began to squeeze.

"I wanted to keep it safe," he managed to say through coughs. "Just in case you tried to choke me in public." Oberon held the pressure for a moment before loosening his grip. Nicky coughed to catch his breath and looked up to see a small dog looking down at them from the hole above them. Oberon leaned back and scoffed. As he did, Pizza Hawk began playing its most classic song, *Another One Bites The Crust*.

"Perhaps you aren't as stupid as I thought."

"No. I probably am. I've just seen a lot of movies. And I know you never bring a knife to a gunfight." Nicky looked up at the man. "You're not like the other ones, are you?"

"What makes you say that?" Oberon said.

"You seem like you want to kill things. Will just wants to kill me."

"Will? Is that what he called himself now?" Oberon laughed as he took a glass of soda and threw the entire thing in his mouth. His teeth crunched on the glass and he smiled at Nicky. "No. I am their king."

"We don't have a king. We're a democracy. I mean, apart from the corporations."

"I don't understand anything that you just said, so just shut up and listen. I want that book. I will get that book. Now, you have that book, so either you can give it to me willingly or I will take it and destroy you. Now, with that in mind, will you help me?" Nicky looked at him and remembered all the bad things Will had told him. He remembered every warning he had got about how trusting people was bad and he should not do it. He could hear those words echoing around in his head. Then he listened as Pizza Hawk began playing his final song; *Take Another Little Pizza My Heart* and knew what he had to do.

"Yeah. Sure. Why not?" And then Nicky accidentally escaped when Oberon slammed his head back into the ceiling.

Chapter 12

THE CHAPTER WHERE NICKY CHASES HIS HAND

It had been two hours since Nicky had escaped Oberon's clutches. It wasn't an intentional escape by any means. Nicky left the diner without issue and assumed that Oberon was right behind him. He hadn't noticed when the giant man wedged himself between the fire exit doors and got himself trapped. He only escaped after a team of employees and fire fighters cut him out, and by that time Nicky was long gone. He hadn't bothered to notice he was walking alone, but by the time he got to Mideo Video, it became obvious. For a moment, he thought about turning back, but then he remembered that Oberon was probably evil, so he decided not to.

He entered, expecting hoards of people to be renting videos—It was almost noon after all. Instead, there was a ragged woman walking her snotty-nosed child through the aisles looking for something to distract him and a shady man standing in the corner wearing a trench coat and smelling like old cheese.

What was most disturbing, though, was Vinny. His eyes were red and bloodshot, and he could barely contain himself from bursting into tears. Also, he wasn't wearing his uniform, which made him look unprofessional.

"What happened? You look awful!" Nicky exclaimed. Vinny

wiped his nose on his bare forearm and turned his tear-soaked eyes to Nicky.

"She left me," he stammered. His lip quivered. His hands shook. He looked the way black liquorice tastes. Nicky had never seen him so upset before- and they'd watched Beaches and Titanic together. Normally his frowns were bored or unimpressed, but this time he just looked sad. It was disturbing. With great trepidation, Nicky put his hand on his boss' shoulder and looked deep in his eyes as only he could.

"I'm sorry to hear that. Who left you now?" Nicky asked. Vinny gave him an expression that seemed to scream, *really?*

"Really?" he repeated, but this time with his mouth.

"I mean, there's lots of people in the world and..." Nicky began, but Vinny shook his head as if to clear his thoughts.

"My wife. She found a big, strong man who took her away this morning. Told me I'd likely never see her again." He stared blankly at the computer screen. "I keep seeing her everywhere. I don't know if I can function like this."

"I'm sure you'll find someone. Plenty of fish in the sea."

"Yeah," Vinny said, still sounding despondent. Then his lip began to quiver as his voice croaked. "She loved fish."

"I mean, so did I last night," Nicky responded, rubbing his still sore neck.

"You're young. I wouldn't expect you to understand," Vinny said, though he was only a few years older than he was.

"You've..." Nicky was going to say something, but was interrupted by the woman and her child. She went to the counter, and the boy looked at Nicky with his big, wet, blue eyes, which matched the shiny green blobs that hung from his nose. He then pointed his tiny finger at him and spoke in a squeaky voice.

"You're going to die," he said. The comment gave Nicky chills down his back. Was this the chilling grip of death?

It wasn't—he had just stepped too close to the soda machine.

Like a bolt, the mother swooped between them and scooped the boy up in her arms before smothering his face with a napkin.

"Sorry. He's going through a phase. You know, death this and kill that. He's harmless. Sorry again. Do you have any kids' movies that won't make him want to kill everything?"

"I...' Nicky began as the boy continued to stare at him with eyes of malice. "I mean, not really. Most of them condone death or murder in some way. But you can find a few options in the comedy section that don't have nudity. Just look for the sticker with the breasts crossed out." The woman nodded as she looked into her purse. The boy continued to stare at him despite his mother's tight embrace. It lifted his cheese dust covered finger and brought it to his throat before dragging it across his skinny neck. It left a thick orange line on his otherwise pale skin as the woman carried him away.

"Are you going to be okay?" Nicky asked.

"I'm breathing. And no one needs to know that my heart is shattered... and that the world is a cold and desolate place full of hurt, pain, and... musicals."

"I'm sorry Vinny. I wish I knew how to help but..."

"It's okay. Thanks for the back rub. I appreciate it." Nicky looked down to realise that his unattached hand had wandered over to Vinny and was currently crawling up his back. When Vinny turned to head into the back room, Nicky reached across to grab his wayward appendage, but it easily dodged his grip. His hand flipped him off and launched itself over the side of the counter. Nicky watched as it raced around the floor, using his fingers as legs. Acting fast, he gave chase and followed the crawling hand into the children's movie section.

"Dammit," Nicky said as he scoured the floor for his hand. He had clearly seen it running around, but had lost It somewhere between the enchanted penguin movies and the never-ending series about orphan dinosaurs. He picked up some of the videos in case it was hidden behind one, but couldn't see anything. He also wondered how his hand could move so effectively without having eyes or ears and concluded that it must be magic. Or maybe he was controlling it? He didn't understand how this worked.

"Come here, me," he yelled. He had never named his hands. It would make certain activities more embarrassing, so he had refrained. Besides, he had always been particularly attached to his hands. He certainly preferred them to his feet, but he hoped that his feet didn't know this.

Then a shadow appeared behind a collection of old cross-dressing rabbit cartoons. He leapt out to grab it, but his hand skittered out of the way before he could nab it. He raced after it, running back to the front where his hand was digging through his pack. Sneaking up, like a clumsy lion, Nicky leapt up and caught it, but his hand was on a mission. When Nicky pulled it out, it clung to the book, which flew out of the pack and landed on the counter.

As Nicky tried to force his hand back onto his wrist, he looked up at the book to see it start to vibrate. Then there was a spurt of black ooze that shot out in the shape of two people. For a moment, the beautiful woman was standing there and Nicky felt his stomach flutter. She was covered in black ooze, which actually looked good on her. Well, he preferred it to the fish scales and grotesque fish face that she had used to mangle his neck. She was about to smile when a sword chopped through her neck and sent her head flying straight into Vinny.

The headless body flopped to the ground. A thick black oil geysered out, and the body shrivelled up like a novelty toy in the oven. The body twitched, coagulating into a muddy, black puddle. It smelled like liquorice.

"Did you just decapitate a woman in my store?" Vinny asked as he held up the woman's head. Nicky had assumed that the woman being headless would have answered the question already, but maybe Vinny was slower than he was. He then turned to see the sword's handler and saw a very upset looking Will glaring at him. Then Will took the sword and levelled it directly at Nicky's face.

"Careful where you point that thing. You don't want to hurt me. Eh, buddy? Eh pal?" Nicky said as he slowly backed up against the fridge.

"Give me one reason why I shouldn't plunge my sword straight through your stupid face." Will spat through grit teeth.

"Because you need me?" Nicky squeaked. He watched Will's mouth twitch. Nicky swore he could hear Will's teeth being ground into rubble. Then he wondered if fairies had teeth the same way that he had teeth. "Hey, do you guys have teeth?" Will paused at this. A part of his brain appeared to short circuit as he remembered who he was dealing with. Glowering, he lowered the sword and turned away as he cleared the black gunk from his face.

"You sucked me into the book," Will growled.

"In my defence, I had no way of knowing what would happen. You should have explained it better." Will turned back with a frown more frowny than his last frown.

"Fine. I'll give you that. From now on I'll explain everything to you, the way I would explain things to a very small, stupid, and unstable child."

"I appreciate that."

"VERY small. VERY stupid-"

"I get it."

"Completely unable to understand the simplest of tasks..."

"Okay, now you're just getting mean." Nicky crossed his arms.

"You smell bad," Will said.

"I let you out, didn't I?" Nicky asked.

"What good does that do when you let out every evil as well?" Nicky paused and looked at Will.

"Are you evil?" Will lowered his sword and looked at Nicky incredulously.

"What?"

"You were sucked into the book. Doesn't that make you evil as well?" Nicky pointed at the sword. "And you do have that."

"I'm not evil. I'm magical. There's a difference," Will said. He walked over to Vinny, who was still carrying the head of the fish woman. Will grabbed it by the hair and held it above him. "Now that... that is evil."

"She doesn't look so evil to me," Vinny said. "Might just be a skin condition."

"Could be! We don't know!" Nicky said. "Are you really willing to take that risk?" Will tossed the head back to Vinny, who caught it, but didn't appear to be happy about it.

"She's not dead. She's a Fae. Give her some time in the dirt and she'll be good as new," Will said. "And right now, we have bigger problems than arguing among ourselves."

"Like what?" Nicky asked. Will pointed his sword at the figure in the trench coat, who was still standing in the corner of the store looking suspicious.

"Like how that man hasn't moved since you've got here."

Chapter 13

The Chapter Where They Fight A Broom

While Nicky had never been the most observant human being, he figured that even he should have noticed that the man had stayed in the exact same spot for the entire time he was there. How long had he been there? Did he need their help? Or was there just something in the R section of the wall that was truly captivating? Even perverts only took a few minutes before quietly moving on.

He followed Will to the man. Will, walking carefully with his sword on high alert. Nicky casually chewing stale popcorn as he tried to hide behind him. They arrived at the man and Will nodded to him to get behind. Nicky, already cowering behind him, complied.

Raising his sword, Will tapped the man with the blunt edge, causing the trench coat to fall to the floor. He wasn't sure whether he should have expected a skeleton, or a man with three eyes, or just a pile of children stacked on top of each other like a tiny human tower- but what he saw was not what he had expected.

"It's a broom," Nicky chuckled. Will turned to him and sighed. It was indeed a broom. It looked like a broom that someone had applied a trench coat to.

"Is this some kind of joke to you?" he asked. Nicky became serious, at least what he hoped would pass for serious.

"No. I'm just stating facts. It's a broom."

"Right. Fine. Well, I guess..." Will sheathed his sword and turned to the front when the broom leapt up and hit him on the back of the head. Will grabbed the back of his head and scowled at Nicky. "Ow! What did you do that for?"

"I didn't do anything," Nicky said and threw up his hands in a 'don't shoot' motion.

"Well, someone hit me and you're the only other one here," he said as the broom leapt up and hit him again. But this time, he saw that Nicky was not the culprit. Nicky smiled smugly when the broom smacked him in the face.

"Ow! It's not funny when it happens to me!" Nicky exclaimed. With a shove, Will ushered Nicky behind him and the two backed their way towards the front. As they did, the broom floated towards them in a threatening manner. As if it was daring them to try its patience. Nicky gulped. He never knew that a sentient cleaning object could be so intimidating, but now he was happy he'd avoided them all these years. "What do we do now?"

"We use the book. But we need to figure out what it is first."

"It's a broom! It's a flying broom!"

"Brooms don't just fly. Something is controlling the broom. Controlling it psychically or carrying it with invisible hands." Will ducked as the broom swatted at them, but didn't warn Nicky. The broom smacked into his face so hard he toppled over. "Watch out."

"Why thank you. So glad you could help me out with that," Nicky snapped as he peeled himself off the ground, rubbing at his wounded face. The broom crashed down on him again, but this time, Will managed to grab it by its shaft. He yanked it hard and the broom burst from whatever was holding it and landed beside Vinny at the front counter. He was still clutching the decapitated head in his hands and was looking shocked. Nicky had forgotten he was there.

Feigning bravery, Nicky walked up to Will and tried to find any sign of the broom holder. "Did you get it?" he asked as Will frowned, moving to where the creature had presumably been.

"I don't know," he said as scanned the space around them. He paced back and forth, looking down and scouring the ground for something, anything, that might have been the thing. But there was no thing. In fact, there appeared to be nothing at all. "I don't trust this. Grab the book." Nicky reached into his pack and pulled out the book when it burst from his hand and slid across the floor.

Will shot him a 'really?!' expression. Nicky shrugged and tried to communicate, 'It's slippery!' but that was harder to do with just eyebrows and sass.

Moving quickly, Will lunged and wrapped his arm around the invisible creature. Nicky presumed it was a neck. He hoped it was a neck. Whatever it was, it did not appear to enjoy being choked.

"How do I do this without sucking you up?" Nicky called out as he knelt over the book to prepare.

"Get behind me! We can do it together," Will grunted as the invisible creature bucked him back. Nicky nodded, and raced behind Will, positioning the book in a way where it would catch whatever he was holding without sucking him up. This was the theory, at least. However, Will looked worried. He didn't seem keen on being sucked back into the paper abyss again, and Nicky's aim was so bad that he rarely used urinals.

Holding his breath, Nicky opened the book and a spew of ink blasted out and covered the creature. The creature itself was a mess of what Nicky hoped were tentacles that waggled and screamed as it was sucked into the book. A few of the appendages tried to reach out and grab hold of him, but they were dragged away leaving only thick, black, inky smears. As the last of the beast was sucked into the book, Nicky closed the pages and Will breathed a sigh of relief.

Will looked at Nicky and did something unexpected. He smiled.

"I didn't suck you up that time!" Nicky exclaimed.

"Good," Will said. "Way to suck less this time."

Chapter 14

*THE CHAPTER WHERE HE SUCKS LESS THIS
TIME*

It was the closest thing to a compliment that Nicky had received so far. He felt good, which to him felt wrong. He wasn't used to doing well. –Actually, he wasn't used to *doing* in general.

With a quick pace, Will returned to the front of the shop, while Vinny forced Nicky to scrub the black goo off of as much of the store as he could. A part of Nicky was frustrated that the goo only seemed to stick to items that would be annoying to clean. The rest of him was frustrated at having to work when he technically wasn't on the clock. Sure, he shouldn't have been in the store in the first place, but that wasn't the point.

As Nicky scrubbed through the store, he decided he would be smart about this new venture. If there was one thing he had access to, it was movies and fairies were often featured in them. Seeking out a few options, he grabbed a film that he hoped would educate him. This one made it seem like fairies were mostly about stealing children and wearing giant codpieces while balancing balls. The clean up didn't take long, mind you, he didn't work very hard at it, but once he was semi-satisfied with it, he went to the front where Vinny was deeply engrossed in a chat with the fish woman's head.

Two things caught Nicky off guard with this. One, the fish

woman was still alive and could talk. Two, Nicky's boss appeared to be showing genuine emotion for once.

"I think she gets me," he said as he motioned to her, or at least to her head, which was propped up on the counter with a diet soda can. Her decapitated body was still splayed on the ground in front of them, but luckily, no one seemed to notice or care. The few customers who came in either stepped over it, around it, or just didn't seem to notice. A police officer walked in the doors, saw the body and then turned back around, mumbling something about it being his day off.

"He's surprisingly deep. And I know deep. I'm part fish," the head said as Vinny smiled at her.

"I'm... happy for you?" Nicky replied, unsure what to say about such a situation.

"Your friend is still on the roof waiting for you, by the way," Vinny said, motioning to the back room. Nicky nodded and tried to smile as he made his way to the ladder that led to the roof.

After climbing the precarious ladder, Nicky stepped onto the roof and saw Will looking out over the horizon. It wasn't much of a horizon as the store was only a single story tall, but Nicky gave Will points for trying, at least. Nicky wandered over and sat beside him and tried to see what he was looking at. He didn't see much beyond the parking lot.

"What are you looking at?" Nicky asked.

"The sky I guess," Will said.

"Ah yes," Nicky replied. "There it is." Will laughed- but not in a mean way. It made Nicky feel at ease for some reason.

Nicky wasn't one for all this 'outside' business. He didn't go out much, there was just so much air and none of it smelled like chips. He preferred to be in spaces that were dark and that smelled a bit like him. But on an evening with a perfect sunset like tonight, he could see why regular people would enjoy it. The sky was a pink so vibrant it was almost unnatural- and the few purple clouds that dotted through it were striking.

"Should I be looking for something specific? I mean, yeah, it's okay I guess," Nicky said. "But I've seen better."

"Yeah. I know. But this one is nice, too," Will whispered. "I don't get to see it often where I come from." Nicky looked at Will and then at his elaborately detailed sword.

"You don't come from the book, do you?"

"No," Will said. "I just watch it as it gets passed around. I can't touch it. I shouldn't even be near it."

"So why are you?"

"Because you're the first one in years who was stupid enough to actually open it."

"But now you get to be on a big impressive adventure and swing your sword around." Nicky pointed at the weapon. "That's pretty cool, right?"

"Sure," Will replied. "I guess you mortals look at these things differently. All I can think about right now are the hundreds of beasts that you unleashed that are out there right now, poised to kill everyone and everything and destroy the world as we know it. Not just the human world- those fae were put in there for a reason. Who knows what devastation they'll bring upon the Faefolk."

"Yeah. I guess I can see how some would consider that a downside." Nicky thought about it for a moment. "But isn't it worth it for their freedom?"

Will looked at him with a look of shock and contempt. "For their... freedom?"

"Yeah. I mean, now they're out there all like, 'Hey! I'm free! Let's go out and live our best lives and eat Italian for dinner and... vote?'"

"That's not really how these things work," Will smirked. "These are creatures more likely to eat Italians than to eat Italian."

"But you like being free, right?" Nicky responded.

"That's different. I'm different. They're bloodthirsty beasts who just want to kill people."

"That doesn't make someone bad. I mean inherently. There are plenty of people I've wanted to kill and I'm tempted to do it often enough when I'm working in retail. Wanting to kill people might just be what makes someone human. Hell, I think you want to kill me on a semiregular basis..."

"Right now, in fact," Will uttered. "These things are not human. They're fairies. They're fae like me."

"What they do with other people in their bedrooms is their own business. You should be more accepting of that," Nicky replied. Will just put his head in his hands and exhaled. "Besides, that big guy was pretty nice." Will slowly looked up at him.

"What big guy?"

"The guy from the movie who I went for a pizza with?" Nicky replied. "The big guy? You must know who I'm talking about here."

"Fifteen feet tall? Beard? Three eyes? Kind of green?"

"Nah. This guy was fourteen feet tall, with a beard. Might've been green though. I'm actually colour blind, so I couldn't tell you."

Will stared back at him. "What colour do you think I am?"

"I dunno. Based on what I know about colour, I'd say... off white? Maybe like an eggshell?"

"And this giant man, this man who was more than twice your height... you went for pizza with him?!"

"Yeah. He wanted to have the book. So I figured why not? But then he got stuck, and I didn't bring it so...-" Will stared at him. Nicky was wondering if he'd forgotten how to blink. "What?"

"And you didn't think to tell me this until now?"

"Why would I? I figured that once he got out from the pizzeria, he'd come and meet us here. Then we could hang out and stuff. I mean, he seemed cool, but—where are you going?"

"We need to leave. Now. Grab what you want and..."

"Why? Look, I think he's coming now," Nicky said as he pointed down the street as the giant man lumbered towards them. "Don't you wanna meet him?"

Chapter 15

THE CHAPTER WHERE HE JUMPS OFF A ROOF

Nicky quickly realised that it was much harder to breathe when Will had his hands around his neck.

"Why are you choking me?!" Nicky croaked.

"Because I can't kill you, so this is as close as I can get right now!" he grunted. Will glared at him with eyes lit with such fury it could light the sun on fire. He brought Nicky very close to his face and spoke with enough ferocity to ensure Nicky's face was wet with anger spittle. "Now I want to make sure you hear me when I say this!"

"I still need to breathe!"

"You will again soon. Now look, that man is not a minor fae! He is a major deity! He wants to kill you and take the book! I have been fighting for decades to ensure that doesn't happen, so you cannot give it to him! Nod if you comprehend!" Nicky nodded, and Will loosened his grip. Barely, but it helped.

"Well then, why did you send it to me in the first place?"

"I didn't! I would never have let them send it to you if I knew how reckless and irresponsible you were!" Will spat. "If I knew why Donn would do..."

"Who's that exactly?"

"No time! Come on!" Will yelled as he began to run across

the roof.

"Do we have to run? I mean, I've been on my feet for a few minutes now and I just feel..."

"Just shut up and run!" Will turned back to Nicky as he jumped off the roof of the store. Nicky raced over and looked down with wide eyes. He pointed behind him.

"The ladder is right there!"

"There's no time for ladders! What are you waiting for? Jump down!"

"You do what you want to, but I'm going to take the ladder! I'm surprisingly delicate!" Nicky called down. Will's face twitched again. "I don't want to hurt my ankles."

"There's no time! Just come on!"

"I'll only be a minute! I swear!" Nicky turned to the ladder when his stray hand crossed his path. It blocked his way and, with a surprising amount of momentum, curled itself into a ball like a spider and flung itself towards him. The amount of force coming from the hand was shockingly strong, and it collided with Nicky's nether-region for maximum impact. The collision wasn't enough to cripple him, but it did propel him over the side of the building. With the grace of a potato sack being flung over a garden wall, Nicky toppled over the ledge with a resounding oof.

For a moment, he felt like his body was acting by itself. It contorted like a cat in zero gravity as he tried to find some balance. His brain registered he was falling- but that still didn't mean he was falling well. For a one story building, the fall lasted a surprisingly long time. Enough time for him to reflect on his life and his choices- but certainly not enough time to regret them.

Then, with the grace of an anaesthetised octopus, he landed on the ground. He was like a cat in the sense that his feet were the first to hit the ground. But once they did, he felt the impact rocket through his body like he was a slinky that had somehow stumbled into consciousness. A strange energy coursed through his body and vibrated him with an extreme rattle. And that was when various body parts blasted off of him and landed in heaps around the space. A hand fell by Will. His shoulder landed beside him. He fell to pieces and found himself looking up at a very sour-looking Will.

"Dammit, man. You need to brace for impact." Will shook his head.

"I thought I did," Nicky replied. "Plus, I think I got the impact part of that down pretty well." Nicky watched as his body parts sprang to life and slowly crawled back to him. His leg kicked his foot towards his knee- His hands collected his pelvis and began to reassemble himself. Even his rogue hand, which he still hadn't named yet, had found a way to reattach itself, giving him the dexterity that he had been sorely lacking for hours now. So if nothing else, that was a plus. Will rushed around the space, trying to help him reassemble, but at this point Nicky was mostly able to move on his own again.

With the various parts of him scattered around, he had become very aware of the tremors getting closer to them. Once enough of him was together, he stood up and stretched as the final pieces reconnected themselves to his body.

"Good as new!" He laughed and looked at his reattached hand with a smile before turning his head to see his other hand ending in a foot. "Crap."

"There's no time to fix that, just run!" Will responded.

Nicky looked down and wanted to argue when Will gripped him by the collar and forced him to run alongside him.

Learning to run with a hand instead of a foot proved to be tricky. At first Nicky was afraid of cutting himself, but soon realised that it was far more likely that his fingers would just get left behind if he didn't slow down. The act of running with his hand made it feel like he was continually slapping the ground and in no time, it had become annoying and painful.

"Don't run so fast. It hurts!"

"I know it hurts, but we have to get out of here before we get got, get it?" Nicky did. He got it. But Will didn't have to be so rude about it.

With little choice to do otherwise—they ran. Nicky wasn't sure for how long, but it felt like ages. They ran for what felt like a short eternity, or the length of time it takes to sit through a political rally. Nicky couldn't be sure, but he knew that it must've been at least a few hours, but he was disappointed when he looked back and saw that they were barely two blocks away from the Mideo Video and barely a minute had passed. Nicky kicked himself for being so out of shape, but the hand-foot wasn't helping matters.

"We gotta find a place to rest," Nicky argued. "I can't run on my hand-foot."

"It's getting late. It'll be dark soon. It's best for us to find somewhere we can hide."

"Pizza Hawk?"

"Not there. Somewhere more private. Somewhere with more security. Somewhere that's open late."

"Like a strip club?"

"No. Not like a strip club. That's a terrible idea." Will

frowned.

"Okay, I got it. Follow me."

Chapter 16

THE CHAPTER WHERE THEY GO TO A STRIP CLUB

It was called the Carousel. Therefore, Nicky wasn't lying when he said it wasn't a strip club because it wasn't. It was an entertainment destination. The entire club had a circus theme. The first thing Nicky learned when he came here was that the rides they were offering were different from the ones he had expected. And a lot scarier.

They walked in as two women named Candy and Sugar were doing a routine on a pole together. Nicky's only thought was it looked extremely uncomfortable, but he appreciated their vigour and dedication to the craft. The acrobatics on display were always exceptional, but what he really enjoyed was the food.

"They have excellent cheesy fries here," he shouted to Will, as they ambled to a table in the front. It was a low table with ample access to the stage. Sometimes the dancers would even step onto the table and dance around for them. Nicky was always annoyed when they did that because they frequently spilled his drinks. At least they offered refills on his root beer, which he assumed made things better.

"This place is unpleasant," Will said. "I do not enjoy it here. It smells like your apartment."

"It's fine. You don't need to watch if you don't want to. Or they might have a man or two here if you like. We can ask."

"I did not come to fornicate. I came here so we can formulate," Will responded.

"What's the difference? I mean, can you fornicate? Is that even a thing you do?" Will didn't respond. He settled into his chair as two more ladies took the stage. These ones were named Chocolate and Caramel. They appeared to be nice enough, but Nicky found them very intimidating.

"That's irrelevant right now. Nicky, right now I want you to understand something..." he began, but was interrupted by a perfectly manicured hand that smelled like soap and strawberry lip gloss.

"Can I get you boys a drink?" a server asked. She was wearing what could generously be considered clothes. Her ample chest appeared to be attempting to shatter what little fabric there was. A less intelligent man would desire to do terrible things in that moment, but Nicky knew better. This time.

"Something strong," Will said. "Something very strong."

"Sure thing, love," she said, and gave him a squeeze on the shoulder. She left, taking her breasts with her, and Nicky couldn't help but stare.

"You shouldn't lust after her like that. You don't know for sure she's a human."

"She works here, so she probably isn't. I've seen what they can do and I've never seen a human woman bend like they do." Nicky took a sip from a curly straw. Will shook his head and scanned the room.

"It's not like that. What you've done... you've unleashed many, many powerful fae folk and they're going to want to play with the person who unleashed them. You're encountering Fae. They're a mystical bunch. They can do things, tricky things. They play with your mind. Like you with that fish woman."

"What about her?" Nicky asked.

Will quirked his eyebrow and smirked. "She charmed you. No one would fall for such a basic glamour spell. She knew the second you saw her as she naturally was, you'd try to leave." Will laughed.

Nicky frowned. "You should be nicer to her. She had a great personality."

Will laughed even harder. "That's a good one!" he guffawed. "Here I thought you were dense, and you pull out a line like that."

"She seemed to be genuinely hitting it off with Vinny," Nicky retorted.

"After I cut off her head, and she had no other choice but to play nice," Will responded. Nicky frowned harder.

"Well, I feel you're being very..." Will held up his hand and Nicky stopped talking.

"Look, you're marked now. They're going to be attracted to you. They know that the only thing that can put them back where they've been is that book. As long as you're alive, they will hunt you until they get that back. You need to be on your guard. They can strike at any time. Even here." The moment was interrupted by a pair of legs clad in impossibly high heels. For a moment, they strut around the table before sitting on the ledge where Will was sitting. Then Nicky noticed the rest of the woman they were attached to.

"I hear you want a 'strong'. Something very strong." The large blonde woman spoke with a Russian accent so thick it wore a muff. "Yvanka will give you strong." She leaned back on the table, tossing her hair in Nicky's face. She lifted her legs up, opened them into the splits and brought them down on either side of Will's face. She clamped tight and Will tried to push away but her legs kept him pinned. Nicky tried to intervene, but the woman pushed him aside with her thick biceps.

"Stop it!" Nicky cried out. "He doesn't swing that way!" He tried to pry his hands between them, but Will was stuck. As Nicky tried to separate them, he grabbed a hold of Yvanka's legs and pulled with all his might. To his surprise, instead of dragging her off of Will, his hands popped off and wrenched themselves between Yvanka and Will's passionless embrace. For a moment they opened her grip enough for Will to take a breath, but Yvanka was very strong indeed. She wouldn't budge and began to squeeze so tight that Nicky could see every vein in her legs pulsing. He tried to get his hands to find a more vulnerable place, but when he lunged forward to help, he felt a large hand clamp tight around his shoulder.

Nicky turned to see the very annoyed face of Oberon staring back at him and gulped.

"Oh. Hello. Is she one of yours?" Nicky asked. Had his hands been attached, he would have pointed to Yvanka, but as they were currently attempting to pull her hair, he wasn't sure the gesture would translate. Oberon also didn't look like he wanted to talk much. He leaned in dangerously close to Nicky and smiled with a savage cruelty.

"Why don't you take a walk with me, little man? I'm not likely to get stuck this time."

"My name is..." Nicky started, but Oberon didn't appear to care and ushered Nicky from the room.

Chapter 17

THE CHAPTER WHERE THEY ARGUE WITH BAD GUYS

Nicky looked at the door with trepidation.

"Your friend is fine. For now." Oberon sneered.

"Oh, I'm not worried about that," Nicky said, without taking his eyes from the door.

"Then what is it?" Oberon queried.

"Why do I get you, and he gets the stripper?" Nicky asked. Oberon rolled his eyes and opened the door where Will was guided in by Yvanka who sat by Oberon's side, a sneer on her otherwise beautiful face. Nicky perked up. "Wait, are we trading?"

Will looked at him with a 'really?!' expression. Nicky shrugged.

"I'm just saying I'm sure I would have appreciated the strong female legs a lot more than him. How were they? I know you don't really know these things, but if you were to wager a guess, would you say they were a five? Maybe a ten? Eleven? Did she shave them? Do fae shave? What was it like?" Oberon pounded the small brown table and instantly broke it in half before turning and rubbing his forehead. Within moments, a scurry of tiny six inch tall fae swarmed in and replaced it as easily as if he had asked for a new pen. This one was a sharp black desk with especially pointy edges.

"Your idiocy astounds me," Will sneered. They were now both tied up on the other side of the hulking brute. It was a private room, which Oberon took up a large part of. His hulking body barely squeezed inside, but he still somehow had space for champagne, a shrimp cocktail and a small pet rock, which was proudly displayed on the pointy black desk.

"Apologies. I will rectify this next time I kidnap you," Oberon said as he attempted to look in control again. Nicky burst into a happy laugh.

"Now that's a relief. Hear that, Will? There's going to be a next time!" Nicky exclaimed. Oberon and Will looked at him, baffled. "For a moment, I thought you were going to kill us."

"Oh. I will. But you haven't given me the book yet," Oberon said. "You promised to give it to me, remember? And I would like to consider you a man of your word. Are you a man of your word, sir Nicky?" Nicky laughed again.

"Oh my no. I'm a horrible traitor," Nicky retorted. "Seriously, just ask this guy. All things considered, I'm pathetic. Honestly, I'd probably sell out everyone I know and love in the world for the right price." This appeared to intrigue Oberon and Will's face was turning colours that a face shouldn't be able to.

"So give me the book," Oberon smirked.

"See... no. I don't think so. I don't see how that benefits me in the long run." Nicky shrugged. "I mean, you can't kill us if I don't give it to you, right?"

"Who says I can't?" Oberon smiled, revealing all his teeth in a menacing scowl. There were definitely more than Nicky had been expecting. "Maybe I'll start with your little friend here."

"Isn't that a thing? The fae can't die? I thought that was

a thing." Nicky turned to Will. Will shook his head vigorously. "You said that was a thing!"

"Oh, poor foolish human. Some of us can die. In fact, by the end of the night, I reckon your friend here will be dead. In fact, why wait?" Oberon raised his hand and lifted it towards Will and suddenly Nicky felt a flush of something in his system. Perhaps it was guilt, or guilt, maybe it was guilt, but he suddenly felt compelled to help.

"Wait! You can't kill him!"

"You keep telling me what I can't do." Oberon smiled. "Yet you're not stopping me."

"You can't kill him, or I won't tell you where the book is." Oberon froze again and looked at Nicky, trying to figure out if he was bluffing or not. Then Will looked at Nicky and frowned at him as he tried to figure out if Nicky was bluffing or not. And then Nicky looked inside himself to try to figure out if he was bluffing or not. The answer, it seemed, was maybe.

"You're bluffing." Oberon got close to Nicky's face and sneered.

"Not at all. I hid the book. Somewhere where you can't find it," Nicky announced. Oberon paused for a moment and reached over to the door to the private room. Soon a woman showed up. This one was named Noodles, and he whispered in her ear. She nodded and left, and Oberon sat back and folded his arms against his chest. When he leaned back in his chair, his head hit the ceiling and he frowned. Judging by the dents in the roof, this hadn't been the first time. "You should be careful of that," Nicky pointed out. Oberon continued to look down at them as he pensively rubbed his beard.

Soon, Noodles returned and whispered something in

Oberon's ear. He nodded graciously, turned to the boys as she left. As soon as she had, he gripped the table between them and flipped it over, sending pieces of fine wine and less fine shrimp all over the room. The pointy table was no more, and within moments, there was a deep red circular table in its place.

"Did you mean to do that?" Nicky asked.

"You're not smart enough to fool me twice. If the book is not here, I will find it myself. Enjoy your stay," Oberon said as he left the room. It took him a moment to shift his bulk through, but once he was out, Nicky turned to Will. To his surprise, Will didn't seem that impressed.

"You don't have the book?" he asked, pulsing with a quiet fury.

"Did I need it?" Nicky asked.

"YES!" he yelled. "Where on earth did you leave it?"

"Well... to be honest, I kind of forgot it back at the video store."

"You forgot it?! You didn't even think to remember about the book until now?"

"We just left in such a rush and I didn't think I'd need it," Nicky replied. Will looked like he was about to explode. "Was that bad?"

"We have to get out of these ropes. We have to beat them there! That's the first place they'll look!"

"Did you forget something?" Nicky asked. Will snarled at him.

"No! Because I'm not the idiot who..." Nicky held up his arms in front of him as the ropes fell down around him. Nicky smiled as he displayed his handless stumps for Will to see. Then his hands crawled over his legs and reattached themselves.

Will sighed.

"Right. Untie me. Let's go."

Chapter 18

The Chapter Where They Take A Hike

The strip club had become more popular since they'd been ushered upstairs. Apparently, the daytime weekend wasn't their busiest time for some reason. There were now strippers in clown ensembles and men of ill repute piling into the stalls around the venue. Luckily, they had an easy exit—the downside was it involved them having to dance across the stage in the process.

Donning a pair of clown wigs and name tags, Alfalfa and Nugget burst onto the stage in a haze, because Nicky knocked over the dry ice machine. Thankfully, getting out through the thick smoke was easier than expected, and they managed with only minimal damage to their egos. However, when asked to strip, Nicky attempted to take off a glove, only to have his hand flop off at the same time. That didn't impress the patrons, who had presumably wished to see only the clothes come off and not the body parts as well.

Thankfully, the chaos that followed served as a good distraction, and the two managed to slip out the backdoor.

Bursting into the street, Nicky and Will began to rush back to the video store, but something stopped him. Nicky could feel a thought bubbling at the back of his mind. This was rare, so he paid attention to it. Then he saw it standing in the street and

Nicky turned to the most useful street invention ever created and knew what he had to do.

"Where are you going?" Will asked, as he stopped running.

"Just be a moment!" Nicky called out.

"We can't stop now! We have to get there," Will urged.

"We will. I just need to use the payphone first," he said as he lifted the sticky receiver. "They may be gross, but at least they're handy. Got a quarter?" Will complied as one does when someone asked you for a quarter for a phone call for fear of being seen as rude. After all, everyone always carried at least some change with them, specifically for this reason.

"Why are you making a phone call now? We have to..." Nicky held up his hand for Will to be quiet.

"Goonies. Goonies. Goonies," he replied and promptly hung up the phone. Will blinked at him.

"What the hell was that?" Will asked.

"That was code. Come on. Let's go meet him," Nicky said as he turned away from the video store and started to head into the worst place in the world: the suburbs. Will tried to follow what was happening, but despite himself, followed Nicky. Will appeared to be confused by a few things, but the biggest question seemed to be whether or not Nicky had formulated some kind of actual plan.

"You damn well better know what you're doing."

"I think I got this one." Nicky was surprised. He sounded assured and confident, two words he could barely spell. He sounded proud of himself. But after a few minutes of walking, his pace slowed and Nicky turned to Will with a look of confusion. "Which way to the woods?"

"Don't you know?" Will asked. Nicky shrugged and Will

pointed at the big green tree lined hill in front of them.

"Ah. Right. Come on," Nicky replied.

"What do we do there?" Will asked.

"We're doing a Goonies. He'll meet us at the entrance to the cave."

"Who will?" Will asked. "Which cave?"

"The most Goonies one. Don't worry. He knows the one." Nicky responded as he entered the trail he was looking for. He knew the path like it was instinct. Soon, the houses thinned out and the ground around them became more mountainous. He would like to have the world believe that he effortlessly ran there, but he was actually carried by Will for the majority of it. His strength wasn't quite what it could have been.

Before long, they arrived at a clearing that overlooked the city. There was a tourist trap destination just south of them that had been declared 'the most cave-like tourist trap in the district' five years running. It wasn't a destination they were particularly proud of, but Nicky had been to their diner multiple times and rated it within his top ten. At least within the district. Although their cheesy fries left much to be desired.

"Here we are. Where is your contact?" Will asked.

"He'll come. Don't worry. You hungry?"

"If you lead us all the way out here just to eat, then I will find a way to kill you," Will responded as he looked out over the horizon. The view was impressive for such a small city with a little lake nestled in the distance. This space wasn't quite far enough into the forest that there was no trace of civilization. It was on the edge of town and appeared as if it was fairly close to a monastery because there were tiny crosses that littered the area.

A twig snapped, and their attention shot towards the bushes on the other side of the street. When Nicky looked up, he could see Vinny waving at them. Vinny motioned them over and, after looking both ways, they joined him.

"You brought the book?" Nicky asked when they were close enough.

"Of course. You used the code word, so I ensured I brought everything with me that could be of use. The bag contains the essentials: your book, cola, a knife, some candy, and floss." Vinnie motioned to the bag that was slung over his shoulder. Will took it and breathed a sigh of relief.

"Thank god one of you has a brain. I was worried..." Will opened the bag and saw the head of the fish woman staring back at him. Will closed the bag again. "Why is she in there?"

"She's a good listener. It's really helping me out knowing that there's someone I can talk to about everything that's going on."

"Yeah," Will said as he gave Vinny back the bag. "Nicky, a moment?"

"It's been more than that." Nicky responded, but followed Will anyway.

"He brought the head with him," Will hissed.

"Awe. Good for him. It's nice to see him getting back out there so quickly." Will grabbed him by the collar and brought him close.

"No! It's not nice! It's a fae creature! Hellbent on the destruction of all humanity," Will hissed. "We need to get her, and many, many other creatures, I might add, some even more beautiful and tempting than her, back inside of the book. What part of this are you not understanding?"

Nicky blinked. "You say some are more beautiful?"

Will exhaled long and slow. "I knew you'd get hung up on that. I don't know why I brought it up. Just listen to me. For your, and his, own protection, we should get the head back into the book. Can you do that for me?"

"I guess so, yeah." Nicky looked back to Vinny, who appeared to be laughing along with the head in the bag about something. Maybe she'd just gurgled something cute, or maybe they were plotting a way to run away together. He didn't want to separate them, but if it was for his own good... he didn't like it, but he'd do it. This was why he always hated Old Yeller.

"Good. Now we've got the book, but you don't know how to fight and you don't have a weapon." Will frowned at him. "We can't fight them with our brains because you're an idiot."

"I resemble that," Nicky retorted.

Will stopped breathing. "Did you mean resent?"

"I said what I said." Nicky crossed his arms.

"Anyhow, I need to figure out a way to get you in fighting shape. Or at least how to get you a weapon. Something, anything, to give you a fighting chance against..."

"Hold on," Nicky said as he peered over Will's shoulder into the tourist trap's parking lot. Sitting in the middle of the lot was the hideous appearance of the world's most awful creation: a brown intrepid. "I recognize that brown car." Nicky frowned as he stepped around Will and peered into the vehicle.

Two figures moved around, silhouetted in the headlights. He watched as a shadow opened the door and stumbled out of the car, laughing. Then another one followed with a gait so awkward it could hardly be described as human. His blood ran cold as a slow fury pierced him.

"Bill..." Nicky growled. Bil froze. He looked up and his face went white. Nicky squatted as if he was a puma ready to pounce and yelled across the parking lot at him. "That better be my mom in that car. And if it is, please don't show me."

Chapter 19

The Chapter Where Someone Dies

"Nicky! Boyo! W-what are you doing here?" Bill asked, his hands in the air as if he was under arrest.

"I could ask you the same question, Bill," Nicky sneered at him. He inched closer, getting lower to the ground with each step. He wanted to see the woman that Bill was hiding.

"Nicky, calm down. I'm sure Bill has a perfectly normal explanation as to why he's here," Will responded.

"Yeah. I'm sure I do," Bill said. Nicky frowned and stood up to his full pathetic height. He crossed his arms and gave a sour face that expressed his *oh yeah?* disbelief.

"Well? What is it?" Nicky asked.

"This is my sister. I'm giving her a ride home," Bill said.

"Well... I know you have a sister, but you were laughing pretty intensely there and I know family doesn't laugh like you were laughing. Well... maybe in Alabama." Nicky sharpened his gaze. "What's her name?"

"Sheila," Bill responded. "You know that. You've met her."

"Once. In passing. And I found her off-putting," Nicky contemplated. Bill turned to Will.

"That's a big word for him. Maybe being with you is rubbing off on him." Bill looked mortified. "Not that I'm implying you two are, uh, in cahoots."

"For crying out loud... I'm just a magical being, okay?" Will sighed.

"Whatever floats your boat, yeah? Now look, I gotta get going back to your mum and I gotta take my sister back to her place, so if you need a lift, I can..."

"Hey boys!" Vinny called out from across the street. "Does that man know his fly is down? You can see everything." All three of them paused before turning their attention to Bill's fly, which was indeed down. You could indeed see everything.

"Goddammit," Bill said under his breath as Nicky let out a yell and lunged at him. Will managed to grab him by the torso, but Nicky's hands flew off of his body and wrapped themselves around Bill's neck. Bill staggered backwards and tried to wrench them off, but Nicky wouldn't have it. He was screaming like a child throwing a tantrum. Or perhaps this was how they always interacted in real life. The line was fuzzy at the best of times.

"Get a hold of yourself, Nicky! Come on!" Will reasoned with Nicky as he held the majority of his body back from Bill. Like a very slow flash, Vinny ran over to try to help how he could, still carrying his lady friend in the bag as he moved.

"You need me to do anything?" Vinny asked.

"His hands! Grab his hands!" Will retorted. Vinny slovenly rushed over to Bill to help him pry the hands off. With much effort, he managed to undo one, and as soon as they did, Nicky's other hand sprung off of Bill and crawled over to the bag. It tossed out the head of the fish woman, who protested with a deep moan as she landed on the asphalt. Then the hands leapt out of the bag, holding the book between them. Seeing the book, Nicky began to laugh as Will leapt out of the way.

"Nicky! Stop them!" Will screamed, but it was too late. They were already acting of their own accord. With surprising ease, the hands opened the book, sending out a thick stream of black oil erupting from the book. Once again, the world was coated with the thick oily black nether-substance and blacked out the world around them. However, this time, the tentacles that belonged to whatever monster that attacked them at the video store were plainly visible as they wriggled their way out of the book. They thrashed and spun around the forest looking much bigger and more threatening than before- each one moving like a drunken, oily tree made of rubber bands. They eviscerated everything that they touched, shredding large chunks of the street and demolishing anything in their path. They hit the car, splitting the body in half like it was slicing pound cake - which technically now made it a sedan. They collided with a tree and in seconds reduced it to splinters. When they got to Bill, before he could even scream, he was sliced and diced like a potato in an infomercial. In seconds, he was reduced to a sloppy, messy pile of human meat. Then a torrential shower of blood erupted, painting everyone in the vicinity in a deep crimson slush like a blood fountain.

Seemingly finished, the tentacles retracted. The oily substance around them faded as the book was closed. The tentacled creature let out a gurgled scream as it was forced back into the pages. With a slam, the creature was no more and the book lay beside the hands. Soon, the only thing that made it obvious that anything had happened was the pile of Bill and the outrageous amounts of blood that coated the parking lot.

In the distance, a police officer approached. He saw them and immediately froze, turned on his heels and walked away muttering something about 'not on my time off'.

Will approached Nicky, who was staring at the carnage in front of them, and was unsure what to do to comfort him. Then Nicky spit out a large chunk of what was once Bill and wiped off his eyes.

"I had my mouth open," Nicky whispered.

"You okay?"

"Did I do that?" Nicky asked. "No seriously. I have no idea what happened."

"You did. Your hands did at least." Nicky stared at the Bill pile as it spurted up a small spout of blood.

"I killed Bill. Oh, my god," Nicky said as he slowly stood up and surveyed the damage.

"It's not your..." Will tried to comfort him, but Nicky turned and waved his stumps in the air eagerly.

"This is the greatest night of my life!"

Will frowned. "What?"

Chapter 20

THE CHAPTER WHERE SOMEONE GETS DUMPED

"I can't believe it! I killed him! I got to be the one who killed him!" Nicky was buzzing. Will was aghast.

"I can't believe you're saying that! You shouldn't be happy he's dead!"

"You don't get it! Now my mom is free! She won't have to be with him anymore! I've just done her a huge favour! I should go tell her!" Nicky exclaimed as he skipped down the street, when Will gripped him by the arm and threw him on the ground.

"There is so much wrong with what you just said," Will said as he lifted his fingers. He counted each point very deliberately by waving the respective finger in his face. "First off, you can't go to your mom without attracting unspoken evils to her. Second, you just killed her husband..."

"Boyfriend," Nicky interjected.

"Fine. Her boyfriend. But that's no better! Third, she probably won't believe you if you told her about all of this, so why bother? Four, you are literally covered in his blood."

"She won't mind. Once I showed up at her house in an ascot."

"I don't care! Five, Oberon is still out there and will try to kill us. For real! Again!"

"He's had two chances so far and failed both times. If this is his track record, then he isn't very good at his job." Will put his bloody hands to his head and shook it in disbelief.

"You're impossible. There's no way to get through to you. We're all doomed," Will muttered. "The only reason you've got away from him is because he wasn't prepared for how amazingly stupid and lucky you are."

"That sounds almost like a compliment, you know," Nicky said.

"It's not!" Will yelled. "I... I need a moment to think. Just... be yourself, I guess. It's got you this far."

"Fine! I will. Because this guy has my back!" Nicky said, intending to motion to himself, but forgetting that his hands were currently occupied still on the ground. He looked down to see them engaging in a thumb war. He was winning.

As Will walked away, Nicky saw Vinny sitting on a log beside the head. He appeared to be washing her face off using one of his socks.

"And so, then they take the Centurion Falcon and fly off to the big planet where she was wearing a bikini. I'm really not doing it justice, but long story short, you'd make a good droid." Vinny looked over, apparently just realising Nicky was there. "Sorry Nicky, didn't hear you. Was just telling Gurgles here about Star Treks."

"Gurgles?"

"It's what I call her. You know, because she can't talk much anymore. Maybe it's her vocal chords dying slowly or whatever. She normally just gurgles." Nicky looked over at her.

"You doing okay... Gurgles?" She gurgled in response. He nodded his acknowledgement. "You okay?" Vinny then asked

Nicky, as he made space for him on the log.

"I'm fine," Nicky said. "I got to kill a man that I hated today. So that was nice."

"Yeah. I can imagine that," Vinny replied. Gurgles gurgled.

"I mean, I feel like I should be sad. Because of all that crazy stuff I did. But I feel good about it. I feel like I did it for the right reasons."

"Well, good for you," Vinny said as Nicky burped. "You okay there?"

"Just feeling a bit strange," Nicky said. "Got a bubbly feeling in my gut."

"Like guilt?"

"No. Not like guilt," Nicky lied. "Just like… What's the opposite of happy? But not, like, the obvious one?"

"It might just be gas."

"Yeah. Maybe," Nicky said. He'd had gas before and this didn't feel like that.

"Well, if nothing else, this adventure has connected me and this lovely creature. I think I'll keep her. If she'll have me."

Gurgles looked up at him with her big fish eyes and gurgled. Nicky assumed that meant something because Vinny leaned down and kissed her. Nicky had to turn away because it would be rude to stare. Not at all because it was really gross to look at.

"Good. Good for you," Nicky said as he looked at the car and frowned. He felt something prick at the back of his neck and realised that something was very wrong. "Vinny. Pack up your girlfriend's head. I think there might be trouble."

"What's up?" Vinny asked as he lovingly shoved Gurgles into the bag and slung it over his shoulder. "Don't worry, babe.

I'll take good care of you," he whispered.

"The woman in the car. She's still in there," Nicky said as his stomach feeling intensified. "Oh god. She saw me summon the tentacle thing with my hands."

"You didn't do that. Your hands did."

"Does that count?" he asked. He looked over at his hands. One of them flipped him off before they both scurried towards Will. "I need you to help me with this. I can't open the door. Can you...?"

"Course. Just help me keep my lady safe."

"I got your back," Nicky said. He stepped towards the car and bravely cowered behind Vinny. When they were a few feet away, the car door opened and a long, smooth, slender leg stepped out. It was followed by a beautiful torso, connected to a dazzling woman who wore very little clothing. Finally, a head appeared with hair that cascaded down her face in a way that screamed 'it does this on purpose'. She looked expensive. To say she was attractive would have been an understatement. She spoke and her lyrical voice was like honey fresh from the hive.

"Hey boys. I seem to have lost my man. Can one of you help me out?"

"Me?" Vinny asked. She nodded. Vinny looked at the woman, then at the bag in his hands.

Without hesitation, Vinny took the bag and threw it away. He raced to the woman's side. She threw her arms around him and escorted him into the back of Bill's car, where she closed the door in Nicky's face.

Nicky looked at the bag and walked over to pick it up. Due to the throw, somehow Gurgles had fallen out, and though he looked for her, he couldn't have known where she had gone.

Somewhere in the depths of the forest, Gurgles rolled to a stop. Mostly frustrated by the fact that she would never find out what happened at the end of The Star Treks. If she'd been human, she probably would have felt hurt or betrayed or unloved. Fortunately, she was fae, so the only emotion she knew was hateful rage. She vowed revenge. Or at least she would have if she could have formed words or done anything else other than be a head.

Luckily, she wasn't alone, as a man in a black bowler cap appeared from the shadows. She gurgled to him, but with a quick flick of his wrist, she was no more.

The man smiled and vanished back into the shadows. It was all very mysterious.

Chapter 21

THE CHAPTER WHERE HE'S NAKED

"Will!" Nicky called out as he made his way along the forest path. "Will! It's dark outside and I can't hold up my lighter. Have you seen my hands? I could really use my hands!" He trekked as the ground became more rocky and the forest thinned out. When the canopy cleared enough, he could look up into a rather beautiful night sky. He wondered how many of the lights he saw up there were other stars that had planets like earth. He figured there were probably one or two, but he could never find them. He didn't really like looking at the stars because they were so big. And they made him feel so small and insignificant. He didn't need stars to make him feel that way. Most things made him feel that way.

After a few dozen feet, he caught his hands trying to climb a tree. With a grunt, he rushed over to them and tried to get them back on his arms. They didn't want to reattach at first, but he outsmarted them once he realised that any hand of his would always attempt to pull a finger. Even if the finger was just a stump.

He didn't have the smartest hands, but thankfully they reattached without issue and he continued down the trail.

He rounded a corner and saw a naked Will sitting in

the forest. At first he thought he was just exceptionally pale in the moonlight, but as he looked at him, he realised that he was glowing. Small orbs of light danced in and out of his body and for a moment, he wondered if it hurt, but judging by the serene and peaceful look on his face, it didn't.

One of the glowing lights floated over to him and began to dance. Curious, Nicky held up his hand and cupped the glowing ball for a moment, feeling it in his hand like a small fragment of electricity. Nicky smiled and squeezed it when suddenly Will doubled over in pain and the small orbs retracted into his body. The glowing stopped and soon Will was just laying on the dirt, naked and covering his groin.

"That was beautiful," Nicky said between Will's pained groans.

"You idiot! That was my testicle!" he groaned. Nicky suddenly felt embarrassed.

"Oh, my god, I'm so sorry..." Nicky said. "I just thought it was pretty and wanted to grab it. The ball. The glowing ball. Not that your balls are... I mean your glowing ball, I guess, was your..."

"Shut up." Will said as he slowly rolled onto his side. "I was thinking."

"You were glowing," Nicky said.

"It's the same thing. It's what I do."

"You glow?"

"Of course. I'm a Will O' The Wisp." Nicky's face flashed with recognition.

"Oh!" Nicky exclaimed. "Wow! That's... what's that?"

"I... never mind. There's no point trying to explain it to you. Can you help me find my clothes?"

"Yeah. Sure," Nicky said as he grabbed what he hoped was a shirt and passed it over to Will. He tried not to stare at him, but he was curious. Before long, curiosity got the best of him and he turned around. He had never seen Will's back before, and he found it odd to see tons of tattoos covering them like a map. Nicky wanted to ask about them, but froze and turned back around until Will was done changing.

By Will's face, you would never guess he was inked. His face gave the impression he was a Mormon, or vacuum salesman, or someone who ate white bread with mayonnaise and no crusts. There was something moderately bad ass about that and it certainly cast him in a new light.

"How do we fight him?" Nicky asked.

"I wish I knew. I was thinking we could talk to his wife, but she doesn't seem to be answering," Will said. "It's possible she's moved on, or at the very least doesn't care that he's out of the book."

"Could she still be in the book?"

"Nah. The only thing in there now is the Kraken. And maybe pieces of Bill," Will said. "I wish I understood more about how the book worked. Last time, you were able to control what came in and out."

"I wish I could take credit for that, but my hands did that all by themselves," Nicky said. "They don't like to listen to me."

"Well, the book must've chosen you for a reason. But why it chose someone so..."

"Charming?"

"Sure, let's go with charming—is beyond me." Will looked at Nicky and frowned. "I think the only thing left to do is to recapture the beasts that escaped and hope that by making the book stronger, that we can weaken the forces of Oberon and hope that there's nothing controlling him."

"That sounds like a lot of work," Nicky said. "Is there an easier option?"

"What? You don't want to run around hunting down the hundreds of beasts that you let escape into the wilderness of this reality?"

"There's hundreds of them?" Nicky asked.

"Likely at least that. It's not the best plan, but it's the only one we got. Now we know where the fish woman is. May as well start with her. I'm not sure Vinny will like that."

"Oh, I'm sure he'll be fine with that. He's found a new woman now. He's making out with her in Bill's car." Will paused before turning to Nicky.

"And you didn't find that suspicious?"

"Not really. She was really hot. I know you can't tell, but..."

"Enough! So a beautiful woman invited Vinny into someone else's car after she'd witnessed said person be torn to bits by a Kraken, and you didn't find any of that odd?" Nicky looked at Will with a confused expression.

"Dude. But she was, like, really hot."

Chapter 22

The Chapter Where They Talk To A Woman

While he couldn't tell exactly what was going on, Nicky knew hanky-panky when he saw it. He had read about it extensively. He'd spied on more than enough cars to know what those curious shadows were doing and had speculated many times as to how it would feel if it happened to him. He could dream at least.

He stayed close behind Will, who held up his sword as he rushed to the door of the car and prepared to strike. Nodding once at Nicky, which had been the signal that they had mutually agreed upon, Nicky crept to the other side as Will silently counted down from three. Nicky had never been good at lip reading, so he just opened the door when Will did, and yelled "boo!" However, no one was more surprised than Nicky when he saw what was happening there.

"What?" the woman asked, looking up at them. In her lap was Vinny, curled into a ball as waves of tears flowed down his cheeks. He was wailing and Nicky took a moment to appreciate how sound proof this car was. Would come in handy.

"What did you do to him?"

"I listened to him. He's got a lot of feelings!" the woman cooed. "Poor darling. Tell me what that vicious woman did to you."

"Twelve years!" he cried out and, as if in unison, Nicky and Will shut their doors.

"What was that?" Nicky asked.

"If you ask me, it looked like therapy." Will shrugged.

"Do you know of any Fae who specialise in therapy?"

"I know a couple, but... wait a minute." Will said as he stormed back to the car and whipped the door open. "Titania?"

"What is it?" she asked.

"I've been trying to reach you! And you've been here gallivanting with a mortal?" Will yelled.

"Well, it looks like I haven't been the only one," she cooed as she opened her door and Nicky offered his hand to help her out. He wasn't sure how he instinctively knew what to do. It was as if just being in her presence was enough to make him want to help her. She walked by, and the smell of her perfume was intoxicating. Nicky looked down at Vinny, who was still crying.

"They leave me! They all leave me!" he said, between sobs.

Nicky turned his attention back to her when suddenly he realised that when he had offered his hand, she had taken it with her, and was currently using it to apply her lipstick.

"I haven't been gallivanting. I've been training!" Will said.

"Well, a lot of good that's done you," she tittered. Nicky tittered along. Will hit him to make him stop.

"He's... special. He opened the book."

"I know. My husband suddenly reappears after I spent so long trying to keep him locked in there? It was only a matter of time before someone was stupid enough to open it up." She turned to Nicky and scratched his chin like a dog. "You're the stupid one, aren't you? Aren't you?" she giggled. Nicky's leg twitched like a good boy, and he barked. She then tossed him back his hand and Nicky caught it in his teeth.

"We need your help," Will sighed.

"Why?" she asked.

"Because we need to get him back in the book. We need to get them all back in the book. Otherwise, life on earth will be destroyed."

She turned to Will with a smile. "You always over exaggerate these things. You said the same thing about the French Revolution. You said the same thing about Norman. You said the same thing about the dinosaurs."

"I was right about the dinosaurs!"

"But life went on. Life always finds a way. These humans are cute, but they could use some improvement." Will frowned at her. "Now don't be silly, boys. I've got work to do. And I want to put these finer human qualities to work. Come now, crying man. Let's get back to your misery. It sustains me," she said as she slunk back into the car and entwined her hands in his hair. "Begone with you," she said back to Will and Nicky as the doors of the car slammed shut all at once. Will looked at Nicky.

"Well, now I know why she wasn't answering," he said.

"Is she always like that?" Nicky scratched his head.

"No. Sometimes she's a redhead." Will sighed. "I was really hoping she'd give us something to use against him."

"Well, we can try this book thing and hope that it works."

"At this point, it's our only option. We just have to come up with a way to outsmart him." Will said.

"Not out smart him! I got it!" Nicky exclaimed.

"What? You got what?"

"I'll out stupid him!"

Will blinked at him. "You'll do what?"

"He'll be expecting us to come up with something intense and clever. Something that would go against his ultimate plan. We know what we need to do to start to lock these magical things up. So let's focus on that and not focus on him. Let's have no plan for him! We'll improvise it! We'll do the stupid thing!"

"That is the worst plan I have ever heard."

"Hey, it's worked against him twice so far. I am the king of accidental stupidity! If anything can make this work, I can!"

Will smirked, "I hate everything about this. But you make a good point. You stupid, stupid man."

"Thank you."

"Still not a compliment," Will said. "And I think I know a good place for us to start."

Chapter 23

THE CHAPTER WHERE THEY HUNT A DEMON

Though Nicky had walked through, and smoked in, this grave-yard many times before, there was something about knowing that a demonic creature who rides on a horse and carries his skull in one arm and a whip made of human spine in the other, that some might describe as 'off-putting'.

"Do we have to hunt this one first? Can't we find a bunny fairy? Or maybe like a squirrel? Can we just go fight squirrels?"

"Keep quiet. He'll be around here somewhere."

"How about pillows? Are there pillow demons we can..."

"No. For the hundredth time, just go with it. We're here to fight this thing and capture it in the book one way or another. You got that?"

"Fine. I got it. But does it have to be like, right now? Can't it wait?"

"It's probably already killed. We can't risk letting it kill again."

"Why not? We've already killed Bill," Nicky whispered, but Will stopped him as they were passing a tombstone of someone named Butts. Nicky tittered at the name. Some things were just always funny.

A creepy fog descended and Will pointed as a lithe, demonic

figure emerged from the shadows. It looked truly terrifying and epic, like it had stepped off a heavy metal album cover. In reality, it was bad ass, but decidedly unfriendly. He looked away when suddenly he began to snicker. Will looked at him with wide eyes when Nicky pointed at the Butts' tombstone and whispered, "Her name was Smelma."

"First off, her name was Selma. Secondly, shut up and get over there!" he said as he tried to escort him to another gravestone before the Dullahan could sense them. Nicky by now was sniggering. He couldn't stop himself as a laugh began to bubble up inside of him.

"Will!" he excitedly whispered. Tears were flowing down his cheeks. "Her name was Smelma Butts!" Will did the only thing he could do and turned Nicky's face so he was facing the tombstone. However, this only made Nicky laugh louder.

"What are you doing?! Are you trying to get us killed?"

"Will!" he said louder than before. "This one's name is Luisa Bigfanny!" Will looked at the tombstone and frowned.

"You gotta be kidding me," he said as he scoured the graveyard for a name that wouldn't make Nicky laugh harder. However, the only names he could find were 'Rex Hiscock', 'Major Woody' and 'Tom'. Figuring Tom would be the best option, he guided him over and planted him safely out of the eyeline of the beast. "You got the book?"

"No. But they do," Nicky said as he lifted his stumps in the direction behind Will. Will turned to see Nicky's hands performing with surprisingly agility as they hoisted the book on top of a tombstone and sat in wait.

"Have you got a grip of yourself?"

"Yeah, yeah, I'm fine," Nicky said through a snigger.

"This one was named Tom," he chortled. Will frowned at him and turned his attention back to the Dullahan. It circled around a few graves before turning back and proceeding back the way it came. "It's just walking in a line?"

"He's got no head. How else do you expect it to get around?"

"I don't know? Smell?"

Will rolled his eyes. In a few moments the creature would be in line and they could strike. As the creature walked past, Will gave the signal and Nicky motioned for his hands to open the book. But they didn't. "What are you doing? Open the book!" Will ordered.

"I can't! I'm trying, but they..." He motioned to his hands with his chin. "They're not listening."

"What are they doing?"

"Cat's cradle?" Will looked over at the hands and saw them manipulating a piece of string between them.

"Dammit. You had one job!" Will spat. Like a rocket, he raced to the gravestone where the hands were goofing around. Unfortunately, this caused the Dullahan to sense him and it pursued. It raised its whip and unfurled the spine before cracking it down so hard it shattered the tombstone of Ms Butts.

"Will! Watch out! He's got a whip!" Nicky called out. He stood as he tried to warn Will, but all that did was to attract the creature's attention. The whip cracked beside him, blasting a cross into pieces. He yelped and ducked down behind what was left of the gravestone when he saw a shadow moving in front of him.

At first he thought it was just a shadow, but as it grew, he quickly realised it was a black cloud. It was dense and foggy and looked like it was rapidly condensing smoke. Soon it began to take a shape as long, spindly arms burst forth from the main body and a pair of glowing eyes began to blink from the swirling clouds. A long muzzle emerged from the front of it and a long black tail from the back as the creature looked ready to tear something apart. Giant teeth glinted in the moonlight as the beast began to growl and hunched down, preparing to strike.

"Uh, Will?!" Nicky yelped as the beast sprung into action, opening its massive jaws as it leapt towards him. Just as it reached the zenith of its height and was preparing to come down, the spine whip collided with it, causing the cloud wolf to burst into nothing. "What the hell was that?"

"I'm a little busy right now!" he called out. Nicky looked over his shoulder to see Will fighting his hands as they attempted to play patty cake. He watched as Will grabbed Nicky's hands and forced them to clamp onto the book and unlock it. He slowly opened the covers just as the Dullahan was approaching Nicky.

Looking up at the creature was staggering. It was colossal from this angle and as it raised his whip, slowly, he knew that this was the end. He had finally stupided himself into a situation that he couldn't stupid himself out of. This was the end.

He looked over at Will just as his hands opened the book and felt a ray of hope. He could catch the beast in the book! They could destroy the shadow wolf, or whatever it was that had lunged at him. He was in the clear!

Then there was a flash of black goo, and Will screamed as he was sucked into the book.

Nicky looked up at the creature and sighed. He was dead. At least he would die in a graveyard, so they wouldn't have to take him far. Then the beast froze and the shadow wolf appeared beside him. They both looked at each other for a second before turning their gaze back to Nicky. Perhaps they were communicating who would be able to eat what parts of him. Or maybe they were dividing him up in their minds to make the most efficient use of him.

"Care for a tea, old chap? You look positively distraught," a voice called out. Nicky blinked.

"Did you just...?" he asked, looking up at the beast, who had not yet lowered the whip.

"Over here, old boy," the wolf said. Nicky turned to him to see what looked like a monocle perched on the edge of his long muzzle. It had dark features and glowing eyes but spoke in a distinct, posh accent. Nicky looked at the creature in shock. "Oh? Shocked, I can speak, are you? I'm a smoke wolf. I can say whatever I want and I will do it well. This is my boy. Chipper. Chipper, say hello."

The Dullahan raised its free hand and waved before bringing the whip down to Nicky's face so he could see all the detail in it. It was a human spine all right. Looked fresh too. Nicky tried to not wonder where it had come from. Perhaps it was Bills.

"Hello Chipper. I'm..."

"We know who you are, boyo. Now come with us. We've got a ways to go. And I require tea," the smoke hound said.

"Don't you have a name?"

"Quite right. In the old country they would call me..." The wolf stood up proudly. "Jammy. You may call me Jam Jam if you wish."

"Okay. Jammy, where are we going?"

"Why the only place to go at this hour to get a decent tea," he said. "Come. Bring your book. You may require it. Also, I believe you left your hands around here somewhere. At least one of us should have opposable thumbs. We mustn't keep them waiting. Chop chop!"

With a strange feeling between curiosity, fear and hunger, Nicky scooped up his hands, grabbed the book and followed the creatures. He wasn't sure where they were going to go, but Nicky felt confident that at least if he held Will close, he would be alright. With no real alternatives, he followed the creatures into the woods as the moon slowly began to disappear in the darkness.

Chapter 24

*THE CHAPTER WHERE THE OTHER ONES
SHOW UP*

Nicky had seen enough bars to know when he was in one, but this was unlike any bar he had ever seen. For one, they served him real drinks, presumably with alcohol. For another, it was crawling with ghosts, goblins and unspeakable horrors. Also, it had chairs! Some with backs!

"What is this place?" Nicky asked.

"It's a safe place, boy. At least for now. Now hop off Chipper so he can grab me a pint." Nicky obliged and Chipper trotted to the front of the bar where a mysterious glowing man with no neck was pouring drinks of a variety of colours. Some glowed, others pulsed, still others exploded in puffs of dust. It was all very neat.

The space was peculiar. Not quite outside, but offering no real cover from the elements, either. Lined with trees so thick it would be nearly impossible to squeeze out and a roof made of plants, flowers and nests. Nicky was unsure if the canopy above them had been engineered or grown into place to protect them from the sky. The space itself was clean considering that the floor was literally dirt and the tables appeared to be rocks covered in runes and pixie vomit. In the centre was a fountain that spurted up glowing green water, but upon closer inspection,

MATTI MCLEAN

was actually just a small demon creature continually vomiting into a pool. While the space was nice, Nicky had to admit that he didn't feel safe.

"What makes this place safe? I don't feel safe," Nicky asked as he passed by a particularly curmudgeonly demon.

"It just is. Trust us," Jam-Jam said. "What would you like to drink?" Nicky turned his attention to the vomiting fountain demon.

"Whatever he didn't have." Jam-Jam smiled and signalled something to Chipper. Nicky wasn't sure if it was anything, since how on earth could Chipper see anything with his head tucked under his arm?

"Come on, boy. Sit. We have much to discuss." Jam Jam said as he hovered himself into a small booth.

"Like what?"

"I was hoping you would tell me. Oberon seems quite interested in you. And you're being guided by your very own Will O' The Wisp? And the book has fused with you giving you this... Unique ability?"

"You mean the hand thing?"

"Yes," Jammy said. "The hand thing. Quite unique. I can say I've never seen a manifestation of an ability quite so unique before. How did it happen?"

Nicky shrugged and removed one of his hands, placing it on the table. A few other patrons of the space took notice and came to watch.

"I wish I knew. It's neat though. The only thing is they have better rhythm than I do," Nicky said as his hand began to do a tap dance. It wasn't very good, but it was infinitely better than Nicky could do by himself. The onlookers offered up a modest amount of enthusiasm for it. Jam-Jam gazed at him with his curious red eyes glowing with profound interest.

"You are certainly a strange choice for such a monumental expectation. How are you coping with it all?"

"Okay, I guess. It's all rather confusing. I don't think I understand a lot yet."

"Well, I imagine that must be a familiar experience for you." Jam-Jam said as he took a sip of a mild green beverage that Chipper had brought for him. Chipper then handed a similar beverage to Nicky, who took it and nodded his thanks. He took a sip of the drink and spit it out in disgust.

"What's in this?" he asked. "It's awful!" He said as he took another sip.

"It's green tea."

"I appreciate the offer, but that's vile."

"Strong words," Jam-Jam said with disinterest. "Such a shame. I was actually starting to like you."

"What?" Nicky asked.

"You have to accept a fae drink, in a fae place, within a fae circle. Did folklore teach you nothing?"

"I mean, my dad died when I was young and my mom..."

"I don't mean like that," Jam-Jam responded.

"I mean she was great, but she..." Nicky did the 'drinky drinky' motion. Jam-Jam looked at Chipper, who shrugged.

"Look, we know more than enough to keep you here forever. You have given us your name. You have sampled our hospitality. You are now our prisoner in this space. Do you understand?" Nicky looked from Jam-Jam to Chipper and frowned.

"No."

"You are now our prisoner," Jam-Jam snarled.

"Oh. Okay. Why?" Nicky asked. Jam-Jam snarled, which was not something Nicky realised that a smoke wolf could do.

"Look... my, how do I explain this? We don't care for Oberon, or Donn, or Titania, or any of the elders. We are a small rag-tag group of gremlins, ghouls, goblins and geists and we are sworn enemies of everyone in the Keith bloodline."

"Oh. Why?" Nicky asked.

"We had a good thing going for a long while. The upper deities fought each other and would hire us for their services. Then the book came and locked up the most dangerous ones and we had to adjust. And we did, but then the elder had to get involved and gave us... Keith."

Everyone hissed at that name.

"Who's Keith?" Nicky asked.

"It's just... I really thought you knew more about all this than you do. Keith was the one who came in and fumbled everything with that accursed book. Man was able to essentially eradicate the fae entirely, and just stopped once he had locked up everyone who would hire us. We've had to form a society of mutual understanding and brotherhood. It's been awful." Jam-Jam looked to Chipper. "I'm frustrated right now. Are you frustrated?" Chipper nodded. "Look, you understand my reluctance to cut to the chase. There's just so much to talk about. I know the others tell me to not play with my food, but you're just so fascinating. I mean, I've never met someone so colossally stupid before. It's really quite a treat." Nicky clenched his jaw.

"I'm getting very tired of people calling me stupid. And also of them trying to kill me. I want you to know I am of perfectly average intelligence." Jam-Jam snickered to himself, and Chipper joined in. He laughed from the hole where his head would be. It was a deep and slow laugh.

"Ha. Ha. Ha," he echoed.

"Come now, boyo. There's stupidity, luck and then there's just dumb luck. And you're just dumb unlucky. A true idiot of your bloodline. Now relax and just let us kill you. It'll be easier that way."

"Screw you guys. I'm out of here."

"Boy, you walked right in here. You drank some of our drinks. You won't be able to leave here now. I'd call it a trap, but I don't even feel like we had to try at all. You walked in of your own volition." Jammy said. Nicky looked around and noticed that even though there weren't a lot of patrons in the vicinity, all the ones there began to enclose on him. If they were going to strike, they'd strike soon. He had to act fast. He had to formulate a plan... Alternatively...

"You know the best thing about having people underestimate you?" Nicky said. "They don't expect you to have dumb luck!" he exclaimed. Everyone froze. Several of them looked at each other, confused. Jammy looked at him with a strange expression that was somewhere between impatience and confusion.

"My boy, is there something that you're getting at here?" Jammy asked. Nicky deflated.

"It's a thing. A tagline? Like something that a hero would call out before he does something that fixes everything?"

"I don't follow. What something are you doing now?"

"This!" Nicky said as he whipped his hands, or more precisely, his stumps, out from in front of him. Jammy looked to Nicky and then to Chipper, as if expecting something to happen.

"Your stumps?" Jammy looked to Chipper, and then to several other patrons around the establishment. Then they all began to laugh. Some pointed at him. Some cackled. Most just roared at the embarrassment they knew that Nicky would be feeling in this moment- but then Nicky smirked.

"Take a look behind you," Nicky responded. Jammy froze, and with great caution, Jammy looked down to see Nicky's hands behind him. They were holding the book and in a flash, opened it.

"Oh, bloody hell," the wolf sighed as the black eruption sprang from the book and flooded the space. Jammy, Chipper and the half dozen other denizens of the bar were splat with the black oil, then dragged into the book. Tentacles of ink surrounded them and captured them one by one. Each patron of the bar disappeared as their screams filled the air. He wasn't sure if they were being decimated or just lovingly corralled, but either way, he didn't care. They had called him stupid. They deserved to burn.

After the torrent, Nicky leaned back and watched as the world began to calm down again. The book began to close and for a moment, Nicky hoped that Will would pop out and help him once again. But once the cover was shut, he realised that he was now alone in the middle of a bog. Still hand-less, he knelt down on the ground beside the book and tried to take a drink from the terrible tea but couldn't. The ordeal was fruitless.

If he was to figure out how to get Will out of the book, he had to have a plan. He had to find out how and where to capture the rest of the Fae folk, how to defeat Oberon, and maybe find a way to tell his mother the truth about his "accidental" murder of her boyfriend without getting into trouble. So he decided to go to the only place he could think of where he might stand a chance. To go back to the place where it all started and figure out exactly what to do to overcome everything.

Gathering his hands back onto his stumps, he left the bar area and intended to go home and sort all this out.

Instead, he went into the nearest bar and drank himself into a blackout.

Chapter 25

THE CHAPTER WHERE HE SLEEPS ON A BOSOM

"I want another!" Nicky exclaimed as he banged his glass against the bar.

Now this was a bar. It was dark and moody and smelled like old feet and cheap beer- despite the fact that he was the only one left here and the beer was expensive. Nicky banged his comically tiny beer against the bar again, this time prying his face off of the sticky surface and letting a single stream of drool roll from his mouth. However, his head proved heavier than expected and thumped back onto the bar in a heap. He'd drank enough that his blood alcohol level was yes.

The bartender came by, lifted up Nicky's head, wiped underneath it and then put down a shot glass to collect his spit. As he closed his eyes, only for a moment to rest them, he felt someone come up to him and sit beside him. A floral scent filled the air as he opened his eyes to see one of the most beautiful women he'd ever seen.

"You smell like misery. Mind if I join..." The woman looked down and saw Nicky before her face turned into a frown. "Oh, it's you."

"Tit mania?" Nicky slurred.

"Titania. And no. It's not me," she said, freezing for

a moment before turning around and leaning on the counter. "What brings you to this establishment?"

"I made Will go in the book." Titania laughed at this. "And then I sucked up Jam Jam and Chipper when they tried to kill me and he didn't come out. And now I don't know what to do. So I got a drink."

"More than one, it looks like." She smirked at him, and the look made his stomach flutter. Like he'd just eaten a dozen butterflies. Which, as it turned out was just an expression. Nicky had tried it once, but that just made him think that sounds had taste.

"No. You're not. I'm drinks," Nicky said as he tried to lean back on the bar stool.

"You're drunk," she said with a smile.

"No. I'm not. Just my head's drunk. If I were to turn myself over, I'd have my feet drunk. But now I just..." he then realised she was alone and frowned. "Where's Vinny?"

"He's safe. He ran out of misery so I needed to go somewhere else."

"He dead?" Nicky asked through a hiccup.

"No. He's safe."

"No. You're not. You're drunk," he said through another hiccup. "What?"

"You need my help getting Will out of the book?" she asked. Nicky nodded. "Well, isn't that a shame? I could help you, but what do I get out of it?" She leaned back and settled her chest in such a way that Nicky couldn't avoid looking at them if he tried. And he wasn't going to try. A part of him wanted to just fall into her, and he had a feeling that she'd let him. But it would likely cost him. He tried to pull away, but it was as if the alcohol in his brain was pulling him towards her neckline like a moth to a flashing "Girls Girls Girls" sign. However, it was doing it very, very slowly.

"What... You... boobs?" Nicky asked. Nicky wasn't looking, but Titania began to smile. He could feel a flood of memories coming back to him. Thoughts of his childhood he hadn't thought about for years. As he was being drawn closer and closer to her, she began to stroke his hair, drawing him in faster. The memories came slapping at his head like a drum. He remembered things he didn't want to remember. He remembered places that he'd forgotten. Dates he'd disappointed. The ending of that awful dog movie. He remembered everything, and all of it was sad.

Through all this, Titania just kept whispering for him to let it all out. Grown men cry. It was okay. At one point he swore he could feel a tear fall from his eye, and she pricked it off his face and shucked it down like it was an oyster. The memories became more and more vivid until he made contact, and suddenly the world went white.

He was six. It was raining and smelled like dirt. He held in his hands a single rose that he had to put on something. He couldn't remember what. He was lonely and scared and everything around him seemed off. He was wearing black, and the building was big and strange. Something he'd never seen before, but there were weird pictures of strange, elongated men in the windows. He was holding his mom's hand, which was weird. She was never this clingy before but now she wouldn't leave him alone.

His eyes itched. He scratched them as he sniffled. His nose was red and hurt from wiping it with his sleeve. His mom kept telling him to stop. He didn't.

He stood over the hole and dropped the rose in. The big brown box at the bottom looked like it was a hundred miles away. The rose disappeared into the darkness. He wanted to follow it. But wait- that wasn't a rose at all-

The men spoke. The rain pelted his little face. He was cold. Everyone was sad. They kept telling him to be strong. He just wanted to play. But he didn't want to play anything he'd played before. He wanted to play a new game. A game he'd never played before. Something that wasn't going to bring up old memories.

Then he was back.

The bar returned. He opened his eyes and realised that half of his body was resting on the top shelf of Titania. He shot straight up and looked at her with big, scared eyes. Was he crying? Why was he crying?

"That was delicious," she hissed. Nicky looked at her as if she had just licked out a small portion of his brain and declared that it was satisfactory.

"What was that?"

"Nothing, my dear. I'm just trying to help you," she cooed. He hated it when women cooed, because he found it totally and completely arousing on levels he barely understood.

"You're not helping. I don't think you want to help me at all," Nicky said as he frowned at her. Her eyes twinkled as only eyes filled with mischief can twinkle.

"But dearest. I am helping. I am helping do the one thing you need right now. I'm releasing you. Now tell me..." he tried to move but found he was transfixed. He couldn't do anything but watch as she spoke and the world around him began to blur. "Tell me about that day."

Chapter 26

THE CHAPTER WHERE THINGS WERE SAD (LIKE REALLY SAD)

Nicky walked down the hall clutching Mr Floofs. It had been with him since he had left the cradle. It would be with him today. He took Mr Floofs and brought him into the dining room where he had hoped his mother would have his food ready, but today, it was Ms Horner. He didn't like her very much, but he knew not to complain today. Today was not a day for complaints. Today was a day where he'd need to be a big boy. Today was the very important day.

Ms Horner smelled like jelly beans and farts. Her smile was always big, and she pinched his cheeks too hard. Her laugh was something between a hyena and an owl with an ominous cackle that cracked through the rooms like a whip. Her red hair was done up today and her makeup was thick. She looked like a goblin. But Nicky didn't complain. He had to behave.

He ate her stale pancakes and wondered how they could be stale already. He went to the living room and sat on the couch while she called someone and made the arrangements. He turned on the TV. He never normally got to watch TV during the daytime, but today was an important day. He watched as a man yelled at a woman who did something with another woman. They ran around a blue stage and jumped on the furniture erratically. One of them threw a chair. It wasn't anything special. He couldn't even pay attention. But he appreciated remembering that he got to watch TV in the daytime. Today wasn't going to be all bad.

Ms Horner took his hand and walked him outside. She licked her hand and smeared his hairs down. He never liked wearing this outfit. He always wondered why he had to have a good suit. He wondered why he needed to have a suit at all. He didn't like wearing suits. No one would like wearing suits. To him, it felt like he had slipped into a giant wool sock that was attempting to eat him alive. He fidgeted and wanted to strip it off, but he didn't. He had to be a good boy. One day was all it took. That's all he had to do.

Walking into the building was weird. He knew some of the people, but everyone knew him. Some commented on how cute he looked. Others said how strong he looked. (He liked those people more) Yet more didn't come talk to him at all. They simply let him be and chose not to let him know what was happening. He didn't seem to mind.

Once he got to his mom, he held her hand all day. She held it so tight he was worried it would break. But at some point, he realised that he was holding her hand just as tight.

He didn't cry. At least he didn't remember crying. Maybe he did because his eyes were puffy and itchy. He wasn't sure exactly what was happening, but it was bad. In his mind, he could see the box in front of him. Covered in flowers that he hated. Wearing clothes he hated. It was a new kind of torture he never knew could exist.

"You're a good boy, Nicky. Promise me you'll always be a good boy." His mother stated it like a question. Nicky looked at her and nodded. She didn't look at him, but he knew that she knew. He would do whatever he could today. He had Mr Floofs to protect him.

Maybe it was the rain that made his hand too slippery. Maybe he had thrown it in and expected that he could get it back, but the last image of that day was of a stuffed bunny falling into a dark abyss. Gravity dragged it down into darkness and he knew that day that some things would never be able to be returned to him. Some losses were inevitable, and others were just cruel. In the end, the only consistent thing was that he had lost something massive.

Then there was only the blackness.

Nicky opened his eyes to find himself in a strange bedroom. There were purple curtains and velvet blankets. It felt great, but after a moment, he realised that whatever spell had been put on him had broken. He turned to see a half-naked Titania sleeping on the bed beside him with a big smile on her face. In her teeth she held a daisy that she smoked like a joint and laid back.

"What was that?" he asked.

"It was good, wasn't it?" she moaned. "I haven't had agony like that in a while."

"You poked around my head. I didn't say you could do that."

"I'm queen of the fae realm. A space you can't even comprehend. You mortals do little for me, so I don't really care what I do with you. If I can get pain like that, I might just keep you around."

"This is what you do? To men like me?"

"No one like you, dear," she said as she played with

his arm. "Smart men. Powerful men. Real heroes. You're just an appetiser. But not a terrible one. At least your agony is fresh, all locked up inside of that stupid little head of yours." Nicky frowned and kicked the sheets off the bed. At least he tried to. They cocooned themselves around his legs, preventing him from getting out at all. He wondered what kind of crazy webbing the bed was made out of.

"Where am I?" he finally asked.

"You're here," she said with a smile. "That's all that matters."

"Well, I don't want to be here anymore. I don't like it here," Nicky said. "I want to go."

"Then go." She smirked. Nicky couldn't help that something was wrong with the way she said that. It was too easy. But then again, he hadn't made it as far as he had by not doing the smart thing.

So he left.

This surprised her and in his last glance at her, she appeared to be making a 'What the fuck' face, but he didn't care. He wanted out and so he left.

He stumbled out of the room, then the hall, and then the house. There were dozens of paths and winding stairwells, but for some reason he was able to find his way out perfectly.

He stepped into the cold and quickly realised he had no idea where he was. Also, he realised, he did not have on any pants.

Chapter 27

The Chapter Where He Gets Lost

The house that he walked out of wasn't one that looked familiar. Although the trees were the same as the others in his area, he didn't recognize any of the layouts. He tried to figure out where he was and realised one thing: It was cold. He wished he had a coat, or another layer, or something more luxurious to wrap around himself.

He stepped out and felt something crunch beneath his feet. He looked down and frowned to see his shoe immersed in a light smattering of snow. It was cold and clung to the tops of his socks in an annoying way. He wasn't impressed. He wasn't even sure that it should be snowing right now- but here he was outside in the cold; pantless and disappointed.

The way he looked at things, he had a few problems. One, his only ally, was stuck in the book, along with perhaps a dozen other monsters and pieces of his stepfather. Two, he had no idea how to get him out. Three, he needed to get new socks because these ones had become soggy.

Hugging his body, he started to walk along the road to where he hoped the town was. It likely wasn't far from here. As the sun was rising somewhere in the distance, he figured it would be a good time to maybe hitchhike with a random person back to the city. If he was walking the right way. He paused and looked both directions, hoping for some kind of sign, but the road was flat and barren.

He sighed in frustration. All this had happened because of the book. The stupid book had done this. At least he still had it. Grabbing the book from his bag, he looked at it, trying to discern something from it that he hadn't caught before. Maybe a detail he'd overlooked? He looked at the cover which had a large, 'DON'T OPEN FOR THE LOVE OF ALL THAT IS HOLY' warning in dark black ink scrawled across it and wondered why he hadn't noticed that when he'd opened it in the first place. He still would have opened it.

He looked across the road to see more random suburbia. He smelled the air, but could smell only the beautiful pure scent of an autumn morning. He frowned. He could vaguely detect the scent of a pumpkin spice latte on the breeze. It was truly hell.

Nicky, while chilly, was still curious and thumbed across the pages of the book. He wasn't sure what he was looking for, but when he felt the small bumps on the edges of the pages, his curiosity was piqued. Pulling the book up again, he concentrated and noticed something odd. There were small ledgers with symbols on the edges of them. When he looked at them, he tried to figure out what the symbols were, but none of them looked familiar. Except for one. He had seen the pattern before but couldn't quite place where. He turned to his hand and wondered whether or not he should take the chance and open the book. His thumb gave him a thumbs up before he realised that he was actually the one controlling it. Thankfully, that didn't deter him. Holding his breath, he thumbed to the page and opened it.

He had expected a massive gallon on the inky black substance to shoot out and cover him, but this time there was hardly a spittle. All at once, Will burst out looking unhappy and landed in the middle of the road. At first Nicky wondered if he was alive and as he slowly lifted his head, he could see Nicky staring down at him.

He then realised where he had seen the image before—it had been a pattern that Nicky had seen on Will's back. A part of him wondered why he remembered that.

"You can't blame me for that one," Nicky said proudly.

"Oh, yeah?" Will spat. "If you could control your hands, we wouldn't have been in this mess."

"I'm getting better. Sort of. I mean, it's hardly an issue now. I've caught a bunch of them since you've been locked away in there."

"I know. I was there." Will said as he got up to his knees and looked up at Nicky. Nicky looked down at him with a sour look on his face. "What?"

"You've got a..." Nicky leaned down and flicked a meaty piece of Bill off of him. Will thanked him as he stood up and looked over.

"Thanks. I guess. Was that..."

"Bill? I think so." Nicky said. "Are... are you okay?"

"Yes. Yes, I'm fine," Will said. "Thanks for getting me out of there."

"Of course. I mean, there were these symbols on the side and I realised..."

"Didn't I already tell you about those?" Will asked.

"It matched your back. I could tell it was you because of your back... your tattoos."

"You remembered my tattoos?" Will asked, looking at Nicky with a strange expression.

"I saw you in the... When I squeezed your testicle?"

"Ah. Yes. That," Will said. "And you remembered?"

"It was... Yes. Yes, I did." Nicky was feeling flustered. He was without pants—why was he feeling so warm? "I just... I wanted you back."

"That... I'm...Thanks," Will said, unsure how to continue. Nicky coughed and expertly changed the subject.

"I think I've got myself a little lost," Nicky said. Will looked around, taking in the area for the first time. He looked around, as confused as Nicky.

"Yeah... what's the last thing you remember?"

"I blacked out at a bar. And then she came in. And then I woke up in her bed. And then I left."

"You... Wait, you left? You just left?" Will asked.

"Yeah? I just used my legs and walked out."

"You just... how? Did you just walk out?"

"I just did." Nicky shrugged. Will blinked at him. Then he blinked again. "What?"

"You... How... I don't know how you managed to do that. You don't just leave sacred fae spaces. It should be impossible to..."

"Man, you sound like Jam Jam. Kept saying I'd never leave the Fae space. But I did. And now they're all in the book and you're not."

"Wait, they're the ones in the book? How on... why did..." Will began, but stopped. "I don't know how you're doing this, but whatever it is, it's..."

"Dumb luck," Nicky said with a smile.

"Very dumb luck." Will then paused and turned to Nicky. "So

if that's the case, which direction should we go?"

"What do you mean?"

"Tell us where to go and I'll follow you."

This time Nicky was the one to blink. "Why?"

"Because whatever incredulous luck it is that you have seems to be helping us out a great deal here. So let's test out your luck and see what happens. Sound good?"

"I mean... Okay- But I think I have a better idea," Nicky said as he ran along the street for a while before pointing up. "How about we just follow the road signs?"

Chapter 28

THE CHAPTER WHERE THEY GO SOMEWHERE THEY SHOULDN'T

Hitchhiking had never been Nicky's preferred method of transport. For one, he found it tacky. For two, he never enjoyed the company of strangers. For three, he was always afraid someone would stab him and take his wallet. Not that he ever had enough money to steal, but he did enjoy the wallet. For four, he could never remember to bring a towel.

This farmer's truck had been big enough for them both to fit in the front, but Will insisted that Nicky spend his time in the back riding with the pigs and ensuring none of them fell out. Nicky didn't mind. He felt at home with the pigs. They understood him.

He wanted to pretend he was okay. But the fact of the matter was right now that all he wanted to do was go home to his mom. That memory of the day was still playing in the back of his mind. He didn't want to have to talk to her about Bill, but he knew that the discussion would come up and he still wanted to go. Something about being a young child again, and standing over what he assumed must've been his father's grave was beyond unnerving. He felt insecure. He felt agitated. He felt like he'd just eaten bad shrimp and had to pay premium prices for it.

The man dropped them off at a corner close to where Nicky's mom lived. It seemed the appropriate space and Will didn't protest, but he wasn't convinced, either.

"I want to know how she's doing."

"She's still alive. Isn't that enough?" Will retorted. "I'm all for doing this, but I do think we need to focus on Oberon and what he's doing. He's out there, probably recruiting for some nefarious reason or another. Maybe it's a good idea for us to regroup somewhere and figure out what we should be doing."

"Do we? Seems to me like we don't need much of a plan," Nicky replied. "Go out and catch the beasts with the book so we can go and fight Oberon, right?"

"It's not that simple, but you're not wrong. I just... I wonder why you're going back to your mothers when you just... Is this a good idea?"

"I'm going to see my mom whether you want me to or not. Are you going to come with me, or do I need to put you back in the book?" Will looked at him. His brow furrowed and his lips pursed into a frown.

"You're becoming a real dick, you know that?"

"I do my best. Now come on," Nicky said.

They arrived at the house in no time. As they approached the door, Nicky could smell bacon cooking. It brought a smile to his face. He knocked and within a few minutes, she opened the door dressed in a revealing nightgown.

"Honey bear, I think I got some extra..." She froze when she saw Nicky and Will standing there. Then she screamed. Then Nicky screamed. Will just turned away, but had he wanted to, he could have justifiably screamed as well. "Nicky! Baby! What are you doing here?"

"I wanted to know how you were..."

"Is Bill with you? I haven't found him all morning. Sometimes he goes for sleep walks and so I cook some bacon to lure him back. He's like a bear that way. Always looking for the honey." She lowered her voice. "I'm the honey."

"I didn't need to know that."

"If you need to, you can go into extremely graphic detail. I'm sure Nicky would love to hear that," Will said as a smile spread across his lips.

"Oh! And I will! I don't mind oversharing. Just ignore the candles. I put them on to put myself into the mood. Nothing gets me hotter than scented candles!" She pointed to one on the counter as they entered. "This one is called Celtic Moon! It smells like Enya and whales. What'll they think of next?"

"I just want to ask about..." Nicky began. "Mom, I-"

"Nicky, why don't you run upstairs and put some pants on and then I can go upstairs and put some pants on, and then we can all have a little chat?" She turned to Will. "You're welcome to wait in the kitchen."

Obediently, Will walked to the kitchen, and Nicky headed upstairs to his parents' bedroom. He reached into his mom's closet and grabbed a pair of what he presumed were Bill's pants. Luckily they fit, but the fabric was stretched. Bill was significantly smaller than him.

In the bedroom, he noticed a picture of his father that his mother left on her desk. He didn't notice it often, and frankly, he barely recognized him anymore. His mother told him he'd been a great man, but if Nicky was any indication of his father, he was okay at best. He couldn't have been a brave man, or a smart man, and definitely wasn't an important man- but maybe he was an okay man. Nicky hoped that one day someone would be able to describe him that way.

"Hey Mom?"

"What's up baby? Are you done in there? Can you find me some pants? You able to grab me a sweety? Can you grab me a sweety or two? I'd love it if you could grab me a sweety."

"Sure Mom," Nicky said as he peeled his eyes away from the picture and turned to the cabinet to grab his mom some sweets. He never questioned how he knew that there were sweets in his mothers 'special' drawer, or how he'd discovered it, but since he'd been a child that was where she kept them. Luckily, it was much easier to grab them as an adult. As a child, he'd had to use all sorts of contraptions to get at them- which considering the wide assortment or special items in the drawer was something he didn't like to think about now.

Despite this, when he reached into the drawer for the sweets, he felt something sticky and wet and instantly wanted to scream. He was then relieved to see what looked like a tiny sea-horse that neighed at him with a trumpet like mouth. He pulled his hand away, and as he did, he realised that the creature had adhered itself to him. Nicky tried to shake it off when his hand dislodged and fell to the ground.

Like a bolt, and carrying his hand on its back, he watched as it scurried into the hallway with his hand in tow when Nicky heard a shriek come from the living room.

"You okay in there?" Nicky asked. He looked down at the stump of his hand and frowned as he chased after the tiny hand thief.

Chapter 29

The Chapter Where They Battle A Tiny Horse

His mother was standing on a chair looking down on the floor as if it had suddenly turned to lava. Nicky looked over to Will, who was holding up his hand with the little seahorse attached. He was shaking his head.

"What do you know about Kelpies?"

"You mean those hideous horses that attract young men and then go into the water and drown them?" Nicky's mom said. Both Will and Nicky looked at her with astonishment. "What? You think I've never read a book before? I read things, Nicky! I'm a good reader! I've read lots of things."

"Well... Good. Good for you," Will responded. He walked over to his mother's aquarium of plastic fish and dropped the kelpie in, still clutching Nick's hand. As it hit the water, the creature began to rotate it around and around like an alligator in a spin.

"Thank you," she responded.

"Is that what that thing is? A Kelpie?" Nicky asked.

"Yes. And it looks like it's trying to drown your hand. Likely won't let go until it succeeds." Will smirked.

"It can't drown my hand! I like that hand! Also, how can it drown a hand?" Nicky said as he held up his stump. His mom looked at it and shrieked.

"Nicky! Your hand! I'll get you a band aid!"

"It's fine, mom. Just a thing that happens sometimes," Nicky responded, trying to calm her down.

"No! I'll get you a band aid! Can one of you boys help me down? It's so high!" Nicky offered his mom his stump, but she screeched. Nicky sighed as Will walked over and guided her down to the ground where she quickly shuffled off to presumably get her son a bandage. As she did this, Nicky watched as the tiny kelpie began to race in circles around the room.

"You should tell her about Bill. You know that, right?"

"I mean I *should*. That doesn't seem like the best idea to me, though. I mean, what harm can it do to not know that your boyfriend is... well... in pieces." Nicky responded. "Besides, we have bigger things to worry about. Won't Oberon be sending goons after us?"

"Doesn't work like that. At least, not exactly. Look, you've got a few beasts back in the book. That's not a bad start. But we're talking untold depths of mythology." After a moment of bucking and twisting and contorting itself in the water, it slowly began to calm itself. Apparently content that it had killed the thing that was never alive, it let go of the hand and let it float down to the bottom of the tank. "I mean, it's not like you're doing a great job. A good job at best."

"I'm doing okay," Nicky responded.

"You're falling for every trap that they're laying down. You keep going back to them and somehow escaping. It's unusual."

"It's dumb luck. I figured it out," Nicky said. Will looked at him curiously.

"You keep saying this, but what do you mean by it?"

"Dumb luck. I'm not the smartest and I keep getting lucky. I've got dumb luck." Will wanted to argue this, but didn't.

After a moment, he reached into the fish tank to grab the hand. He threw it to Nicky, who tried to attach it, but found that he couldn't yet, so he just stuck it in his pocket.

"Anyway, on that note, I guess our plan is to..."

"Hang out here and make sure my mom is okay?" Nicky asked.

"No. I was going to say we go out there and hunt the Faes that pose the biggest threat first and work our way down."

"Come on now. I'm sure no one has even noticed," Nicky said. Will smirked at him and went to the front door. "Where are you going?"

"I just want to take a walk and do some reconnaissance. When I come back, we make a plan. This way, I can give you some time to talk to your mom about everything that you need to."

"Like Bill?"

"Especially like Bill. Be safe, alright?"

"But I don't want to talk to her about Bill."

"Tough tenders! Go in there and tell her, or I will!"

Chapter 30

The Chapter Where Mom Is Wise

"Mom? You decent?"

"Just about baby! Come on in!" Nicky opened the door to his mother's bathroom and saw her hair full of curlers and a thick green goo on her face.

"I thought you came up here for a bandage."

"Oh I did sweetie, but then I couldn't bring myself to go back out there without freshening up. You don't mind, do you?"

"No. I guess you've got big plans today?"

"Just going to go out with Bill later. He didn't come home last night so I may have to go to the police station soon. He's probably locked himself in a drunk tank again. He does that more often than I'd like to say."

"Listen Mom, about Bill..."

"Now don't start Nicky! I know you don't like Bill and for the love of me, I don't know why. He's a sweet man. He's devoted, and he loves my figure! You don't know how rare it is to find someone that loves you like that. He's a real catch. I adore him to pieces."

"Right. Well, about the to pieces part..." Nicky tried to say, but looked up at his mom spraying enough hairspray to obliterate the ozone into her mane.

"Don't give me that look. The higher the hair, the closer to heaven. They taught me that at church."

"Yes mom, I know. But I need to talk to you about..." Nicky said. "You like Bill, right? Like, you like him, like, a bunch?"

"Oh, yes, dear. And I know you'll never feel comfortable enough to call him Dad, but I think you should. You'd do good to have a dad like him."

"I had a dad, Mom." He smiled as he imagined what a dad-mom would look like. "And I had a Bill. But now,"

"Where'd you start to become a fan of all this Celtic mythology, anyway?" his mom asked.

"What do you mean?"

"I mean, not every day that you find out your son's hand is attached to a Kelpie. I mean, I never expected them to be so tiny. Like a tiny little seahorse. A sea Kelpie. What a hoot!" She pronounced the 'h' with extra emphasis.

"That doesn't surprise you?"

"No, honey, not at all. I mean, I've known about all this stuff since you were a boy. I get that's what you get when you're married to some kind of ancient druid." Nicky blinked at her as she threw away the last of the can of hairspray before grabbing another.

"He did what now?"

"Oh yeah. Your father was into all kinds of druidic things. That's why we were married in the nude. And why we went to Stonehenge so often." She smiled. "I mean, when that Redcap came in through the window, I thought I would die from laughter. The last time I saw one of them was when me and your father went to Duart castle and one of them tried to eat off his arm. It was so cute. And now, hey! Look at you! Missing your hand!

Oh right, here, let me reattach it for you." Nicky held up his hand and his stump and watched as his mom held her hands up. She then grabbed his hand and put it against his stump before slapping it and waggling her finger at it. Obediently, the hand complied and reattached itself. He wiggled his fingers in surprise. Then she took a band aid and put it on just to show she cared. "There, good as new!"

"Mom... That was amazing!" Nicky's head flooded with questions, but he reached into the bag and pulled out the book. "Do you know this book?"

"Oh, my god, yes!" She chuckled as she grabbed the book from his hands and began to stroke it like an old friend. "I wanted to use this book as our wedding album! Funny story, turns out this book is filled with hundreds of terrible mythological beasts. Turns out the only mythical beast in our actual wedding album is your Gram Gram! Ha!" She smiled as she looked at the book. "I joke, but she really was the worst."

"Mom, I may have let out the terrible creatures that were inside of there," Nicky said. "And then the book bonded with me."

"Oh, well yeah. I figured as much," his mom said. "I'm not like you, sweetie. I'm not a complete idiot." Nicky frowned when his mom looked up at him and put her hand on his cheek. "Oh baby, don't be sad. You've got so many other qualities. Like that one time you got my VCR clock to work for a bit."

"I only changed the hour."

"Well, it was right twice a day. That's not bad!" Nicky smiled as she turned back to the mirror to fix her hair. "Now get going downstairs. I think your little friend is coming back soon and I want to get a drink in before he does."

He hesitated. He wanted to tell his mom what had happened. For a moment, he even debated telling her about Bill. But thinking better of it, he just kissed her on the forehead, that tasted like hairspray, and then went back downstairs.

Chapter 31

The Chapter Where They Talk It Out

Will burst into the house like the Kool-Aid man. In his hands he held a newspaper.

"What's that?" Nicky asked.

"What does it look like?" he asked as he spread the paper out on the counter.

"A shirt for the homeless? Unfinished origami?" Nicky shrugged.

"Never mind. Forget I asked," Will said as he whipped the paper into his hands and started to read. "Calamity ensues as five buildings in the downtown area face massive damage. Here's another article talking about a missing dog. Here's another talking about a pile of flesh that they suspect was a person. And I quote- A massive unknown blast of energy erupted in the downtown core. Unsure whether or not these mysterious events are connected, but their suspicious nature is leading many to suspect that it's the end of the world."

Nicky looked at him expectantly. "Is it?"

Will frowned. "It kind of is. The point is what you're doing isn't invisible. It's out there in the world affecting people. And this is just the start. If you're not careful, we're going to be in a heaping helping of terror as the Fae slowly tear this world apart."

"Well, if it's slow, doesn't that mean we still have time?" Will hung his head and watched as Nicky's mom stepped into the room. She was holding her long claw-like nails up, trying not to touch anything as they dried.

"Did I miss anything?" she asked.

"Will is just showing me how I destroyed the world," Nicky said. His mother smiled and pinched his cheek.

"See? And all those other people said you'd never amount to anything. Destroying the world is such an achievement. I'm so proud of you," she said. "Will, can I get you something? A sparkling water? You want some mead? You fairy people like that, don't you?" Will looked at her suspiciously.

"You have mead?"

"Of course. Why wouldn't I? I used to be married to a druid, you know. He loved the stuff. Practically all he drank. I'll get you a cup," she said as she wandered into the back. Will turned to Nicky with a confused look.

"Oh yeah. Turns out my dad had big ties into this stuff. Turns out mom knows all about it." Will looked at him with an incredulous look.

"And you didn't think to tell me?!"

"Um, I'm pretty sure that's exactly what I just did, no?" Nicky smirked. Will hung his head and shook it. He always seemed to be in a mix of disbelief and perpetual frustration, but at least Nicky was learning. Or at least he thought he was learning, and that seemed like the first step towards actually learning things.

"Right. I suppose I should know better than to expect you to tell me these things," he sighed. "Look, maybe this is a good thing. Maybe your father is the one who set all this into motion?"

"I doubt it. I mean, I guess it's possible. But why would he be going after Oberon and Titty-man?"

"Her name is Titania and I don't know," Will said. "I don't know. I mean, I keep thinking I know something and then it turns out that you're either keeping something from me, or you know too much, or you know too little…"

"That last one."

"It still doesn't help. None of this actually helps unless we know how to defeat him. If he's even the one we should be after. If Oberon was really trying to go after you, why hasn't he made a move? What is he really wanting to do here?"

"Well, what if this is easier than we think? I can just catch him in the book, right?"

"He won't just go back into the book."

"But he came from the book. Maybe he wants to go back. Maybe we won't even have to trick him or anything?" Nicky enthused.

Will was about to respond when a Redcap flew through the window, sending glass everywhere. It scurried around the room causing chaos, but was very bad at doing so as it was very small. As the Redcap was about to smash a plate, Nicky opened the book. The tentacles lashed out, latched onto the creature, and sucked it in.

"You're getting good at that," Will said as Nicky looked at the book in disbelief.

"I guess so. I don't know. I just kind of reacted."

"Well, I'm still here, so that's a point in your favour," Will said as he looked around the room. He had a pensive look on his face.

"What's wrong?" Nicky wondered.

"I just got a weird feeling. That was a really strange thing for a Redcap to do. They're hiding creatures. They don't like to be seen. They prefer to stay in the shadows. Why would it just burst in here like that?"

"Maybe it wanted to scare us?" Nicky replied.

"Were- Did that just scare you?"

"Not at all. Not even a bit. I'm not scared. You're scared." Nicky looked down and saw a small piece of paper.

"Look," Will said as he bent down and grabbed it. They looked at each other and shrugged. Most likely had been attached to the redcap.

"What's it say?" Nicky asked. Will handed over the paper and Nicky frowned. "What language is this? I don't think I've ever seen it before." Will looked at it and flipped the paper around.

"It's English."

"Fascinating..." Nicky remarked as he looked at the letters. Then he frowned. "I can't read this handwriting. What does it say?"

"It wants you to come to a safe place to meet with Oberon."

"Oh. And that's a bad thing?"

"That's an incredibly bad thing," Will said.

"Why? He can't seem to outsmart me."

"I don't think that should be your takeaway from this right now."

"Why not?" Nicky said. "We meet. I walk away unharmed. I've walked away from him multiple times. And from Titty once. They can't touch me. I'm invincible!"

"Once again, I feel like that's a very bad takeaway from all this."

"I'm going to meet him."

"Over my... Look. You can't. Okay? You just can't. Don't..." There was a flash and Will looked down to see that Nicky had opened the book at him. "Oh, you son of a..." There was a flash of black ink and then he was gone. Nicky tucked the book under his arm, went and kissed his mom on the forehead, and then went off to meet Oberon.

At that moment, he realised he had no idea where he was supposed to be going, but he did suddenly have a craving for cheesy fries.

Chapter 32

THE CHAPTER WHERE HE GOES BACK

"I feel like I should have told her about Bill. Does that make me a bad person for not telling her? I mean, it's not like I'm lying... I didn't tell her anything technically incorrect, so really, I should be in the clear. What do you think?" Nicky didn't enjoy the strip club, but he knew it was the place where Oberon would most likely show up. And this time, he was prepared. Across from him, sitting in the booth, were two women: Liquorice and Gouda. He wasn't sure if they were listening to him, or if they had just been here to take advantage of an empty booth away from prying eyes.

"I think you weren't very smart for coming here," a voice called from behind him. He turned around to see Yvanka. She gestured and the other two girls left, leaving her alone with NIcky.

"Are you here to talk?" Nicky asked.

Yvanka didn't answer, and instead said, "You got a lot of balls coming here."

"Thanks for noticing. I just want to talk to Oberon."

"He don't want to talk to you," she said in a thick voice. For the first time, he noticed that she appeared to have two bat ears that stuck out of her head. He wondered how he had missed that the first time.

"I think he might, when he finds out what I'm offering," Nicky said.

"That's cute. Got a reason for me to not kill you right now?" she snarled. Nicky grabbed the book and lifted it up.

"I mean, I can think of one."

"You think he's still interested in that book?"

"Of course he is. I may be dumb, but I'm not stupid."

"Well, even if he is, I don't think he's one to be making deals at this point. Good luck getting close enough to him to be able to pull another one of your tricks."

"Yeah, well, I had planned something more elaborate, but maybe now this will just have to do." Without missing a beat, Nicky opened the book before Yvanka could react. She tried to jump back, but within moments, the vortex of black ink surrounded them in their thick tendrils and dragged her kicking and screaming into the book.

"That's why. Now go and get me Oberon so I can…" He looked down at the book and frowned. "Oh, wait." He looked around the bar, which was now silent and covered in thick, oily ink. Everyone looked disturbed and severely confused. Several screamed for help.

Not noticing all of that, Nicky called out to see if someone could hear him over the relentless pounding of the music. "Does anyone else here work for Oberon? I want to make a deal!" He looked around to see if someone was responding, but no one did. "Anyone? Like even a loser or something?"

"It's him!" someone called out. "Get him!"

"Oh, perfect!" Nicky exclaimed. "You see, I'm here to…" he began, but then someone threw a bag over his head and the world went dark.

Chapter 33

The Chapter Where He Comes To

Wherever he found himself after that was not where he'd been previously. He could tell that someone had put a bag over his head and moved him, but he wasn't sure how long he'd be bag-headed for. Instead, he awoke in the black sack and sighed. At the very least, this bag wasn't plastic, so that was good.

When the bag was removed, he was once again sitting opposite Oberon, but this time, at least, he was in the woods. He could tell because it smelled distinctly different to being inside. Also, it was outside. It didn't matter, because Oberon once again took up most of the space. Nicky smiled at him and waved.

"Hey, buddy! How have you been keeping?" Nicky chirped. Oberon shook his head.

"What do you want?"

"You want the book, right?" Nicky held it in front of him. "I want to give it to you." Oberon quirked his eyebrow. He quirked it so hard it almost flew off of his face.

"I don't believe you."

"Why not? Look at me. I have the book. Isn't that what you wanted?" Oberon frowned.

"I don't know what game you think you're playing with me,

but I'm not interested in whatever trap you're plotting. Put that book away. We've got no need for it right now."

"You don't? I thought it was this big important thing for you."

"It is. But we have more urgent matters right now. We no longer require you."

"Require me? You needed me? Why didn't you just ask me to join you?" Nicky said with a frown. Oberon frowned back at him. His face was frownier.

"We did. You imbecile."

"I'm pretty sure I'd remember if you did. And you didn't," Nicky said. "The only person who wanted me to go with them was Will, and he's been a spoil sport since I first opened the book. Telling me we had to go fight the creatures that came out of it. So I got rid of him."

Oberon was intrigued. "You did what?"

"Will. I put him in the book. He was annoying."

Despite himself, Oberon appeared to smile at this. "You are annoying."

"So I know what it is to be annoying and to have someone annoy you. Don't you know how that feels? The annoyance of having someone ask you stupid questions over and over again? The annoyance of having someone repeat the same thing to you time and time again? You know how annoying that is? No. How could you? Who could annoy you? You're the one who..."

"Stop. For the love of all that is good, just stop." Oberon's face became serious and scratched his chin. He looked like he was considering something. "I feel like you are planning something. But I have also proven beyond a shadow of a doubt that you are the idiot you claim to be."

"I try to be truthful when it comes to my stupidity. I'd hate for people to be surprised by that-"

"But..."

"I do like buts."

Oberon smirked once again, despite himself. "You think I would accept you after all you've done?"

"I think you have to. I mean, you want the book and I have it. And you've proven you can't kill me. Not by traditional means, at least."

"You have proven yourself to be resilient," he groaned. "Like a resilient little cockroach. An annoying cockroach that just doesn't die."

"I am choosing to take that as a compliment."

"Very well. Give me the book." Oberon stretched his hand across the table and laid it down. Nicky looked from his hand to the book and smiled.

"Okay." He lifted the book up and placed it in Oberon's hand. However, when he did, his hand detached and went with it. Oberon tried to pry it off and grit his teeth. He tried to pry the fingers off one by one, but they wouldn't budge.

"Leave your hand with you," Oberon sneered.

"I can't," Nicky said with a shrug. "I'm serious. I can't."

"What do you mean, you can't?"

"Well, since the book bonded with me, or whatever, this happens anytime someone takes it. It's like my hand has a mind of its own and just goes with the book. Just try to ignore it. I can make do with one. This is the one that I use to... ' Nicky paused. "Shave."

Oberon looked at Nicky's unshaven face and frowned. The brute attempted to pry it open, only to find that Nicky's hand kept preventing it. He tried to open it any way he could; dropping it, tearing it, he even tried with his teeth, but each time the book held tight. He looked at Nicky and clenched his teeth so tight that he was sneering.

"I do not know what it is you're trying to accomplish with this, but you shall stop."

"I wish I could! If I could, I would keep my hand. Thank you very much!" Nicky said. Oberon looked at him in disbelief. With an annoyed look, he turned to Nicky and pointed his long, strong finger at him.

"I will find a way into this book. And you will help me."

"Sure. I mean, I could open it for you. As long as I don't have to read it, I'll help however I can. Unless it's a lot of work. I'm not so good at work myself. It's like one of those annoying things I was talking about before it just..." Oberon snarled at him before getting up and walking away.

"You're coming."

"Is that a question or a statement? Two very different meanings."

"Just follow me and I won't kill you."

"You couldn't kill me if you..." Nicky started, but a crazed look from Oberon stopped him. "Right. Sorry. I'll be quiet."

"I'm preparing for a battle," Oberon began.

"Oh, is this going to be like a long monologue or something?" Nicky asked.

A long monologue followed. Oberon was prepping his fae folk to battle a superior evil known as Donn. Nicky wasn't sure what this meant, or why Oberon chose to share in iambic pentameter, but he tried to pay attention at least. As far as Nicky could tell, he had a feeling that the people around him weren't going to try and eat them, and for him, that was enough.

Chapter 34

The Chapter Where He Talks To Hooters

"What do you know about death?" Nicky asked. He had thought when Oberon claimed to be 'putting him to work' that he'd be given something to play to his strengths. Like accounting, or modern dance. Now he was sat in a field overlooking what was supposed to be a battleground, but was still just a tiny soccer field in a park. Sure, there were a few creatures around him gathering supplies, or drinking, or having sex with each other, but he didn't care about that. Not right now. He had a plan to execute. He wasn't sure what that plan was fully, but he knew that at least it was important.

He sighed as he laid down on the dirt. Nicky looked over the field as several others gathered around a fire on the other side. Frustrated, he stewed in his own bad thoughts. Looking down at his stump, he frowned. He had thought Oberon would at least return the book when he realised what a pest Nicky was, but as of yet, nothing. He'd have to try harder to be more annoying.

"I know enough to know that you don't want to know too much about it," the owl responded. He hadn't expected the owl to be so eloquent, but here he was after several minutes of talking to it and was pleasantly surprised by its wisdom. "Also hoot," the owl hooted.

"But... I mean, death is just so permanent, you know."

"Yes. I am aware. Also, hoot."

"I mean, I guess I wasn't expecting to feel this way. Sure, I killed him, and sure, my mom doesn't know... Do you know what it's like to have to carry this kind of secret? I mean, I'm not sure what I'm doing. But I had to leave there, and I knew if I was going to figure out what was actually happening, I had to find Oberon because maybe..." he said. The owl looked at him and flapped its mighty wings.

"You're doing something. That is better than sitting and waiting and doing nothing." The owl said again. "Also, hoot."

"Why do you do that?"

"Just a thing we do as owls. It makes us mysterious. Also hoot."

Nicky pondered for a moment. "Do you think I did something wrong?" Nicky asked.

"Well, from what I can gather, your plan was to ignore your friend and get captured by the only person who you know isn't on your side."

"Yes. Something like that."

"Yes. I would say you did something wrong. Hoot."

"You think I'm doing this as a way of avoiding talking to my mom about Bill? I mean, he was torn into a thousand pieces. It was pretty gross. But also kind of awesome in a heavy metal way. It made me want to appreciate heavy metal, but I just hate the music so much."

"I can understand that," the owl said. "Maybe it's a part of something bigger. Maybe even better. But guilt will always have a way of coming back and biting you. Also hoot."

"Maybe." Nicky looked back to the camp. Oberon was drinking from a keg. A few other creatures were wandering around like drunks on a doorstep.

"So you're a fae, right?" Nicky asked.

"Of sorts, yes. All woodland creatures have access to the fae realms. Plus, I talk. That should have been a good tip off."

"So you know someone named Will? I mean, Will-O-The-Wisp?"

"I do," The owl said. "He was my boyfriend. Of sorts. He was a hoot. Hoot."

"Interesting," Nicky exclaimed. "I didn't think you would be his type."

The owl bowed, then flew away into the night, leaving Nicky by himself. Nicky exhaled. He turned back to the men standing around a fire. What had started as a mini get together between Oberon and a few of his thousand closest minions had descended into chaos and revelry. Nicky wasn't sure what had caused this to escalate into such a feast, but long ago they had decided to stop trying to get into the book and instead were more interested in taking shots and smoking whatever herbs they wanted to.

He laid his back against a tree. They really seemed to enjoy singing as their off-key chanting echoed through the space. He had never suspected giant men of loving pop divas, but apparently it was more than enough to soft rock their world. Their crooning voices were becoming louder and more annoying as he tried to get some shuteye which annoyed him to no end. He opened his eyes and frowned at the stump of his hand, but then realised there was someone laying beside him.

"Just ignore me," a gentle voice whispered.

"Okay," Nicky said, before realising who he was speaking to.

Titania was lying next to him, but didn't even seem to care that he was there. She was just staring across the field at Oberon and his cronies.

"Hi," Nicky responded. "You're not here to make me sad, are you?"

"No. Here I find my own sadness," she whispered.

"Why is this?"

"Just reasons. I don't want to talk about it," she responded. Then she immediately followed it up with, "If you ask me anything about it, I don't think I could possibly tell you anything worthwhile."

"O-" Before he could finish, she continued.

"It all began with our falling out before this chaos. He got locked in the book. I thought he abandoned me. I was distraught. I was troubled. I was a woman scorned. So I did what any reasonable woman would do, and I put a few spells on the book and cursed a few bloodlines. You know. All very basic silly, interesting and ordinary stuff when you think you've been left on your own."

"You did what now?"

"I did so much. And more. I did even more than that. A lot of the bad things in the world I'm actually responsible for. You know late fees? I made those."

Nicky gasped. "You heartless bitch."

"It's not my fault. I was a woman in love. What do you expect someone to do in such a situation?"

"More?" Nicky questioned. "I have to be honest. I'm not sure I expected anything from you. I don't even really know you. Why are you telling me all this?"

"Well, you are planning on locking him in the book again,

right?"

Nicky hesitated. "The thought crossed my mind. But I don't have anything solid yet." Nicky replied. "He's got my hand, though."

"Well then, you're halfway to your own victory. Wait until he's asleep and then lock him inside."

"I don't want to have to..."

"Good. Good talk. You'll do great. I know it," Titania said as she looked up at Oberon one last time with a smile on her face. "I do miss him. Shame. He looks so good when he's full grown. Now, you get out there and take care of him. Good luck, darling." And with that, he was alone once again. He tried to rest and push the thoughts of their conversation into the back of his head, but it was no use.

"What do I do?" he asked no one. No one responded. He gurgled and sat up, looking back at the group. They were still gallivanting around the flames, but at a much slower pace than before. He gathered what little courage he had and began to walk across the area to where Oberon was sitting on what looked to have once been a tree. He didn't want to have this conversation, but he felt he had to. He'd spent enough time on the sidelines. Maybe it was time to do something else. Maybe. If it wasn't too much effort.

Oberon hardly noticed him approaching until he was practically sitting on top of him. Nicky waved up, and Oberon frowned.

"What?"

"I want to talk." Nicky said. "Somewhere we can talk about stuff in private."

"Like what?" Oberon slurred. Nicky sighed and looked at the stars. He hated that he had to ask for what he had to ask next.

He silently hoped there would be some other way to make what had to happen be a thing, but he was stuck.

"So, you're like a god of death, right?" Nicky asked. Oberon looked at him for a moment, seemingly bemused. He leaned forwards on his tremendous haunches and nodded.

"That's not far from the truth. It's not true, but there are parts of truth to it."

"Good. Because I want to know if you have any kind of death powers."

"What of it?" Oberon queried.

"Well, frankly, I need to know if you're able to help me. If not, then I'm afraid you're no longer useful to me."

"And what do you want me to help with?"

"I need you to un-kill someone. I need you to bring someone back."

Chapter 35

THE CHAPTER WHERE HE TAKES CONTROL

"The answer is no," Oberon said as he took a large swig of whatever he was drinking.

"You don't know the question," Nicky responded.

"Death is death. What's done is done. There is no undoing what death has done. Not even by his number one."

"That's no answer. I've killed and un-killed Will at least three times by now."

"Being locked in the book is not death. Death is so much more than you or me. It is so much more than everything."

"But you are a spirit of death, no? Isn't that what you said?"

"I have parts of death in me. But nowhere near enough to do what it is that you are asking me to," Oberon said. "Let sleeping dogs lie. Let the dead stay dead. I don't want to take any part in bringing someone back."

"But it can be done, right? You can bring someone back from the dead?" Oberon shook his massive head.

"I told you that I don't want any part in it."

"Then I suck you back into the book until you're ready to help me," Nicky said. Oberon turned to see his loose hand levelling the book at him in a sinister way. Nicky never realised he could have such a sinister-looking hand before, but here he was, surprising even himself. Oberon turned to him and smirked.

"Do your worst. I'm half into the bag. I won't try to stop you. But good luck talking to the next guy if you wanna experiment with death magic."

"What do you mean, the next guy?"

"If you want me to help you, I can. I'm not saying I will, but I can. The man you want, the one who can bend the realm between his fingers, he's the one you wanna talk to and I can take you there. I'm not saying I will, but I can."

"You're an asshole, you know that?" Nicky said.

"Up to you. What'll it be? Suck us up or find the big demon by yourself." Nicky looked up at him and tried to make up his mind. On the one hand, he could figure out what to do to battle this beast. On the other hand, he could try to do something even he didn't think he could be capable of.

"I'll think about it," Nicky said. He turned to leave when Oberon just laughed at him. His deep booming voice shook the ground.

"Cowards always run!" Oberon yelled when Nicky froze. He was many things, but he was only sometimes a coward. He snapped his fingers and a shot of black erupted from the book as his hand opened it. Oberon was caught off guard as a swarm of ink surrounded him and catapulted him into the book. There was a massive wind as his frame was shrunk out of existence. Nicky lifted his stump as his hand scurried back to his arm and resettled itself onto his hand. The book closed slowly as Oberon tried to claw his way out like a cat that accidentally jumped into a bathtub full of regret. He wasn't screaming, just laughing maniacally as the others in the camp took notice.

Nicky turned to the crowd unafraid and held the book over

his head. He bellowed as the menagerie of creatures looked to him with a combination of hunger, confusion, and fear.

"Listen up dick bags! From now on, I own you! You've seen what I've done to your leader and you know what I can do to you. From now on, you follow me. Anyone who doesn't want to is welcome to spend their last days in the book. Now we're off to find the big bad that can bring back someone very important to my family back from the dead. But first, who wants to point me to the nearest, most private tree? I chugged an iced tea and I've had to go for like five hours now."

Then, ducking into the forest, he pulled out the book and opened it to a very familiar page and just prayed that the one inside would be in a forgiving mood.

Chapter 36

THE CHAPTER WHERE HE'S COVERED IN GOO

"Your ex says hi, by the way," Nicky said. Will was covered in goo that stuck to him like honey and fell to the ground in thick, wet drips. His face was contorted and whereas before he only looked like he was turning red with rage, now he actually was. Nicky had just spent the past few minutes calmly discussing what had happened, and the entire time Will hadn't moved. He had stood, covered in thick goopy goo, without moving anything the entire time. His stillness was almost impressive.

"I have no words right now," Will said, opening his mouth just enough to hiss the words through his teeth.

"You're not still mad at me for locking you back in the book again, are you?" Nicky asked. Will finally turned to him, moving only his head and his shoulder twitched.

"Why would I be mad? You just locked me back into a prison without my consent, after I expressly told you not to. After you expressly told me you were going to do something so beyond insane that it would be irresponsible for me to let you do it in the first place and..." Will paused and looked around. He slowly moved around and examined the area he now found himself in. He did not look impressed. "Why are we here?"

"Because I joined Oberon."

"You did?" Will asked.

"Not really. Just for a bit. And now I caught him in the book and we don't need to worry about him anymore because it turns out he couldn't help us, anyway."

"Help you with what?"

"Oh. I may have wanted to bring someone back from the dead. But he couldn't do that, so I sucked him into the book. And he told me that the only one who might be able to help was someone else, so now I'm looking for the big bad to help me."

"You're looking to... Nicky..." Will shook his head, sending snotty globs of ink showering around him. "What you're saying is insane."

"Thank you."

"No. I mean, it's completely insane," Will said as he clenched his head. He looked like he was about to explode. "Why? What made you think any part of that was a good idea?" Nicky shrugged and looked at the book.

"I mean I got him. So it kind of worked out."

"But why? And what brought about this want to raise the dead? Why are you wanting to raise the dead?"

"Because... reasons," Nicky said. Will gripped him by the shirt and shook him very hard. He yelled at him and then shook him again. And then he did it again just to ensure that Nicky was well shaken.

"That doesn't help!" He finally yelled once he was coherent enough to do so. Nicky took a moment to deliberately wipe the spittle from his face.

"I had to!"

"You didn't! You don't! You can't go after him!" Will said as he threw Nicky back. Nicky wiped off his arm from where the thick goo was stuck to it.

"You didn't say anything about me meeting your ex."

"I don't care about my ex!" Will yelled as he walked over to a tree and sat against the bark. He slid to the bottom as his brain looked to comprehend everything that was going on. He buried his head in his hands and screamed for a good minute. Once that was done, he calmly sat back up, leaned his back against a tree, and rubbed his face. "How was he anyway?"

"Good. He's an owl."

"Yeah. He is," Will sighed. "You're an impossible challenge, you know that?"

"I do my best."

"I can't believe that you're still alive. Everything you do. Everything about you indicates that you should be dead. You must be either the luckiest person I ever met, or the world seems to want you to succeed in ways that I don't understand."

"Which do you think it is?"

"I don't know. Both? This whole dumb luck business you won't shut up about?" He chuckled to himself. "God. God dammit."

"Yeah..." Will looked up.

"So you want to go to Donn and talk to him about bringing someone back to life?"

"Donn, eh?"

"Yes. Donn. Darnus. Hades. Goes by lots of names. The big bad, as you say." Nicky perked up.

"Satan?"

"No, not him. I hate that guy."

"You think he'll help me?"

"No," Will said, but then paused. "But the way things are

going, I wouldn't be surprised if he did." Will exhaled for a long time and shook his head. "I don't know if I can properly explain this, but Nicky, you are beyond anything I've ever encountered before. Your odds of surviving this long are so impossibly low that I'm amazed you're still standing. So if there was anyone who was going to be able to do this then..."

"So, how do we find him? Is there some kind of phone book for you people?"

"What do you mean by you people?" Will said with a frown. Nicky paused.

"You're not a people?" He shrugged.

"Look, you want to talk to this guy, we will talk to him. But first, we're going to need a few supplies.

Chapter 37

THE CHAPTER WHERE THEY MAKE CONTACT

"You sure this is a good idea?" Nicky asked as he held the tin foil satellite dish above his head. Their materials were crude, but workable. He was sure that if he bent himself the right way, he could get HBO.

He watched as Will glowed underneath him. He tried not to look at Will's naked bits but was finding that harder as time went on. Turns out that when he glowed, he also happened to look incredibly attractive, which was very frustrating and strange for Nicky to admit.

"You'll be fine. Just don't fall or die," Will called up. He was shining with his glowing orbs clustered around him, looking like fireflies on speed. Nicky looked up at the sky as clouds billowed around him. Everything about the day was getting more intense. The sky churned and pulsed with energy as the moon was blotted out by shadows. Bursts of electricity shot through the air, hopping from cloud to cloud like insane sprinters seeking shelter from the sky.

"How do I do that?" he called out as he felt the wind blast against him. It was picking up fast, and the longer he was standing there, the stronger it became. He took a breath and extended his arm further.

"We need to get it a bit higher! Can you do the thing?!" Will called out. He motioned to his arm, which made Nicky look at his own arm before realising what he was saying. Nicky took his arm and broke it off, which at this point was a painless, normal thing, and raised it as high as he could in his other one. "Yes! Yes! That's good!" Will exclaimed, and Nicky looked down at him. He was smiling. It was so rare to see that he'd almost forgotten how well put together Will was. His pleasing features were glowing, and not just in a literal sense.

"Is it working?" Nicky asked as a bolt of lightning struck a tree next to him. The blast was so hot he could feel the burn on his face. His mouth hung open as he looked down and started to wave his arm. "It's too close! Too close!"

"Don't worry! This is good! We need Donn to hear us!"

"Do you know how loud those are? I'm not okay with how loud they are!" Nicky screamed. He wished he had a free hand to wiggle in his ear, but for now, he'd just have to live with them ringing because he couldn't use his hands to take his ears off.

"You're through! Send your message!" Will called out. Just as he did, a light burst from the dish he was holding and a shape that looked something like Nicky appeared in a puddle beside him. Will had warned him that it would be reflective in bodies of water, but he hadn't expected to look so miserable in it. He wished he'd taken some time to do his hair because even though he was just a black shadow, it was still driving him nuts seeing how messy it was. His mother would be ashamed.

"Hey there!" Nicky began.

"Oh, my lord..." Will uttered under his breath.

"I mean, hello. There. Donn. It's Donn right? or Darnus? Whatever. God, that's so informal. Like having a god named

Henry or Brendan or something. Sorry, I digress, but it's still kind of a stupid name." Nicky cleared his throat and tried to look intimidating. "I am the one chosen by the book. I am the one who has been guided to you, and I will be the one to capture you. Unless you offer me what I seek."

"And what's that, boyo?" Nicky turned around to see an impish man in a black-and-white striped suit and a purple fedora appear beside him. The shock of his sudden arrival was enough to knock Nicky out of the tree and send him falling directly into Will's arms. Will immediately stopped glowing and Nicky realised that he had a glowing ball stuck in his mouth. Removing it as discreetly as possible, he wiped it off on his pants and gave it back to Will.

"Do I want to know what this is?"

"Probably not," Will responded. They both looked up at the man, who was smiling down on him.

"Is that him?"

"That's a part of him. He must be here to talk. Hope you're up for trying to convince him," Will responded. The man in the hat floated down and smiled at them. He had a crooked smile that made it look like his face was half done. His eyes were small and beady but also the most insane blue he'd ever seen. They looked like they were rotating around, which made him look almost hypnotic. He was dressed in the finest of polyesters, and had a smug look on his face.

"So, you're the boyo who's been going around kidnapping some of my Unders, huh?"

"I don't know what that means. But I've put some monsters in this weird book I got," Nicky said, showing the man the book. He clocked it, but didn't appear to be too interested in it.

"That's all very well and good. Reminds me of a tome that was made many years ago. You're the idiot who unleashed them?"

"I'm glad you've heard of me," Nicky said, sounding almost proud. "I heard you can bring back the dead?"

"I never said that. You don't even know who I am," Donn said.

"Are you Donn?" Nicky asked.

"I'm Donn. But I'm not all of Donn. Consider me his nice side. I'm here to make a deal. Someone else will be by to collect." Donn looked over and appeared to notice Will for the first time. He smiled at him and gave him a wink. "Good to see you again, pretty boy." Nicky felt a weird twinge in his stomach when he said that. Something was strange. Something was off. Was he feeling something that he'd never experienced before? It seemed possible. This wasn't happy, hungry, horny or hupset- or any other feeling that started with H. That made it new territory.

"We want to make a deal," Will stated. "He wants to make a deal."

"Are you a part of that deal?" Donn asked.

"He could be. Would that be a good thing?" Nicky asked, but Will slapped his arm.

"You're not volunteering me for anything," Will said. "Especially not with him."

"You sure? I can put you to good use," Donn said. "You remember the fun we used to have? Want to go back to that place?" Nicky looked at Will and suddenly realised that he didn't want Will to leave. He couldn't just abandon him now. There was something about him that made him want Will to stay.

"Who do I need to talk to, to do this whole reversal of death thing?"

"You want all of Donn. And that's going to be substantially harder to get,." Donn said as he fiddled with the fedora like it was a stimulated nipple.

"Tell me how," Nicky said.

"I'll tell you in your dreams," Donn said with a laugh. Nicky frowned.

"I thought you said..."

"I did. You need to fall asleep and then I'll tell you. Or at least a part of you," Donn said before waving his hand in front of his face and disappearing into a puff of smoke. Nicky turned to Will and shrugged.

"I didn't realise he meant that literally."

"Well, I can definitely tell you he will be there when you fall asleep. Although you may not enjoy what you see. I have no idea what to tell you to expect, and I can't protect you in there."

"Yeah," Nicky sighed. "Here's hoping it's not too hard in there. Why do you protect me, anyway?"

"Because I have to," Will said. "And... because, reasons."

"Oh. Okay," Nicky said. "What are they?"

"Must we go into that now?"

"Why not?" Nicky asked. "But I mean, if you don't want to, I guess I can stop."

"Please do," Will said as he started to walk away before pausing. "Why do you suddenly care?"

"Because I'm wet and cold. And I like talking to you. And I'm starting to feel bad about all those times I put you in book jail. So I want you to stick around."

"Even when I yell at you?"

"Well, considering that's about all you do, I would say so."

Nicky chuckled.

"You're the biggest pain in my ass I've ever had."

"I bet you've had bigger things in your ass." Nicky laughed before realising what he said and turning a deep pink. "Oh, I mean... sorry. I'm just not used to such-"

"I'm fine. It's fine. I guess we have to find a place to get you to bed, huh?"

"I guess so. But... one thing first..."

Chapter 38

The Chapter Where There's A Rainbow

Nicky wasn't sure what possessed him to go here, but in the rain and the storm, the setting seemed appropriate. Standing over the grey tombstone, Nicky noticed so many things about his father that he hadn't seen before. Like his birthday, and his font. And the fact that he had 'devout druid' listed on it. That would have come in handy if he'd seen that before.

After what felt like an hour, Will came over and stood beside him. He took out his sword and tapped on either side of the stone before bowing his head. He said some strange prayer that Nicky didn't know and he watched as a small flower popped out of the ground by the stone.

"Did you do that?" he asked, pointing at the flower.

"Tradition to pay respect to the warriors who came before us," he said.

"Do you think he was a good druid?" Nicky asked.

"I couldn't say. I suppose he must've been," Will said. "Morality is more of a sliding scale when it comes to these things. There are some things that warriors embrace, and there are others that they do not."

"Are druids warriors?"

"I mean, they are as much as you are," Will responded.

"Did you know him?"

"No. But if he's anything like you, I probably would have hated him."

"I suppose so." Nicky nodded.

"Is he the one you want to bring back?"

"No. He's not. There's someone more personal."

"Vinny?"

"Is Vinny dead?"

"When did you last see him?"

"He was crying on Tiatnia's... well... her Titania's."

"And you've seen her again and not him?"

"Yeah..." Nicky thought about this.

"Oh. Well. I'm sure he's fine. He's definitely..." Will paused and looked like he swallowed a gallon of concrete. "He's probably fine."

"Great..." Nicky sighed. "But no. Not him."

"So, you're seeking to bend the rules of nature to revive someone from the place of the dead and it's not your dad or your friend?"

"Correct."

"Well, that's not exactly a small feat."

"It's a stupid thing to try to do."

"Leading me to believe that you're the only one who could do it." Will said. They both laughed. Will smiled at him, and Nicky suddenly realised that he wasn't turning away.

"You're looking at me different." Nicky said.

"I guess I'm just seeing you in a new way. One that I still want to murder sometimes - but at least this time in a nice way."

"And you've always known you were... different?" Nicky asked as he did something that surprised even him. He smiled at Will.

"I'm a Fae. We don't look at things like gender or sexuality as solid things. Everything is fluid."

"Hence your ex being an owl."

"He was also an owl, yes." Will shrugged. "And there are some things that even we don't understand about rules and laws of attraction. But I can see that what you're doing now is out of love. Or something like love. Maybe a toaster or something that you really like, but at least a really strong want."

"I want my mom to be happy. And if that means-" Nicky began, but Will interrupted.

"You're seeking to raise Bill?" He looked shocked.

"Is that so surprising?"

"Actually yes. I wasn't expecting that," Will said with a smirk. "Would it be weird to say that I'm proud of you?"

"Probably. But I'm just a little bit weird, so that works," Nicky said as he turned back to the tombstone and sighed. "I don't really remember anything about him. But when she gave me whatever that was, it brought it back so vividly in my mind that I realised that there's so much more out there. I could feel my mom's loss and I felt guilty. I felt awful over what was happening. I knew there was nothing I could do then, but this time. This time, the least I can do is help."

"I feel like my wisdom is rubbing off on you."

"Well, some part of you is." Nicky chuckled and then turned away. "Sorry. It's not coming out right. I'm not coming out right."

"Is there something you're trying to tell me?" Will asked as a smirk crossed his face.

"No. No, I'm fine," Nicky said, blushing even harder, but soon realised that no matter how hard he tried, he couldn't take his eyes off of Will. "I'm good. I'm really good."

"I bet you are," Will said with a smile as he closed the gap between them. Before Nicky could protest, Will put their lips together and Nicky felt like his entire body was on fire. Electricity ran through his body as his world began to spin. He felt light-headed and dizzy and his knees buckled from the suddenness of it, but Will had no problem keeping them up.

"You taste better than your ball," Nicky said, pressing himself tightly into Will as the rain began to clear.

Chapter 39

The Chapter Where He's Asleep

"Took you a while to get here, but I knew you'd come, eventually. Mortals can try to keep me waiting, but eventually you all need to sleep." Donn said with a smile. He was now wearing a top hat with a gold tooth. He didn't look menacing, but he did look awesome. He had to give credit where it was due.

"Sorry to keep you waiting. I don't remember falling asleep."

"You passed out. After three whole minutes of rigorous love-making," Donn said with a chuckle. "I hope you enjoyed it."

"It was- a new experience. One, I'm a little foggy on the mechanics, but a good experience nonetheless." Donn smiled at him and guided him across the void they found themselves in. There wasn't anything distinctive about the space except for a shiny black floor and a general haze that filled the air. They walked until they found themselves beside a business room table and rolling chairs. Donn motioned to one.

"I trust you have a proposition for me. Something I can't refuse?" Donn said with a smile.

"I hope so," Nicky said. "I need to bring someone back from the dead, and you're the only one who could help me."

"I suppose I might be, yes. But that's besides the point I'm trying to make. You're offering something for me, right? Something titillating? Something I can't refuse? Something that will blow my pants off with such a vengeance that they'll land in your mother's nightmares?"

"I can offer you free rentals any weekday from Mideo Video. I can offer you a fresh TV from my place. It's got a great picture."

"How's the audio?"

"Good!" Nicky said quickly. "Well, it's okay, but it can be expanded to surround sound. How many movies do you know that can do that?"

"Many," Donn said with a smirk. "And it doesn't matter because your offerings don't interest me. When dealing with a devil, it helps to pay them in something they can use."

"Like what?" Nicky asked.

"Dealing in death demands death," Donn smirked. "Is that something that you think you'd be willing to sacrifice? You got anything you need to trade?"

"I... you want me to deal in death?"

"That's the cost. Are you willing to pay the price?"

"I don't know," Nicky responded. "I don't think I can kill anyone..."

"Else, you mean." Nicky looked at him curiously. "You killed Bill."

"Right. Well, actually, he's the one I want you to bring back."

"That's adorable," Donn said. "He's become more pudding than man. Do you really expect me to be able to bring that back to life?"

"Why not?" Nicky asked. "I thought you were all powerful."

"No one is all powerful. There's a limit to even the most powerful of magic. Even though I am strong, you're not just talking about bringing someone back. He's been dead for over a day and his body was torn to shreds. I'd have to reassemble him and then breathe life back into him. That's a mighty powerful ask, and I'm not sure you'd be able to handle it."

"Oh. I guess you're right. I didn't realise you weren't able to reassemble people. I thought you were stronger than that."

Donn frowned at him. "This isn't one of those situations where you can use reverse psychology on me. I invented that technique and I can tell when it's being used against me."

"What is that now?" Nicky asked.

"Your reverse psychology?"

"Buddy, I couldn't even spell that," Nicky said with a chuckle. "But seriously, it's good, right?"

"You're a strange man. And to be honest, I think you may genuinely be as dumb as you're pretending to be."

"Oh, I definitely am. Just don't tell anybody. I don't want everyone to know."

"Your secret is safe with me. But I do want you to consider doing something for me. I'm not saying I'll perform that action for you, but I'll be one step closer to considering it."

"What's that?"

"Unlimited rentals for a week with no late fees." Nicky looked at him with a frown.

"That's impossible."

"I have faith in you. I trust you'll be able to do it. I expect it even. I can't wait to see what plans and schemes you can come up with next."

Chapter 40

The Chapter Where He Wakes Up

Waking up with an arm around him was a new experience. It felt nice in a very strange way. He was facing a wall which didn't look familiar, and he felt a body grinding up against his back, which also was new.

For some reason Will didn't feel normal wrapped around him. He felt cold. Nicky tried to sneak out from under the cover, but the second he moved, Will pulled him back as small balls of light flicked off of him. Nicky had to be sneaky and move slowly, or he would never escape the delightful clutches he found himself snared in.

With the careful movement of a lethargic caterpillar, Nicky shimmied down the bed. For a moment Will loosened his grip and Nicky thought he could escape, but then Will found Nicky's arm and grasped it as a koala would cling to its branch. Getting an idea, Nicky just popped off his arm and made his way to what he hoped was a bathroom.

When the lights came on, he looked at himself. The motel, which is where he presumed he was, was small but surprisingly clean. Only a few cockroaches scattered when the lights came on, and none of them looked bigger than the ones he would find back in his own apartment. It felt like home. But that's when he looked in the mirror and frowned.

He still looked like himself, but he was lost in thought. He had questions. Lots of questions. Lots of big, deep questions that left his brain reeling. What the hell was going on between him and Will? He'd never felt this way about anyone, and up until a few hours ago, Will had hated him. Yet here he was, awoken from fresh coitus and contemplating a deal that he'd made with Donn, a literal devil. Presumably. He was still unsure about a lot of these Fae situations. He mulled it over in his brain. The Fae... Was the Fae doing this to him? What was going on here?

With a deep breath, he looked at himself again and tried to straighten his hair, but it remained adorably scruffy. Surrendering, he slunk back to the bedroom. His brain was too wired for sleep, but maybe this motel had a minibar. Before he could get that far, he saw Will sitting at the edge of the bed. He was naked, and he looked good. He was glowing again, which made him look almost angelic. If an angelic being could be jacked.

"Hi," Will said.

"Hi," Nicky replied. It was awkward, but neither one of them seemed to want to point out how awkward it was. Whomever pointed out that it was awkward first would lose the challenge. Whatever challenge it was, Nicky wasn't about to lose. "Mini bar?"

"Go ahead. I can understand if you need it."

"Thanks," Nicky said as he walked over to the small mini bar and pulled out a clear beverage of what he hoped was vodka. He popped off the top and took a drink. He then clapped his tongue a few times as a field of stars burst across his vision.

"I think that was rubbing alcohol," Will pointed out.

"It's delicious," Nicky squawked as the liquid burned his

throat like fresh kerosene.

"You want your hand back?"

"Keep it. It's yours. I don't need a hand," Nicky said as he tried to hand the small bottle to himself, only to forget he had only one hand right now, and shattering the bottle on the floor. Will slid to the end of the bed so he could be closer to him. Nicky pulled away. Will smirked.

"You don't have to do that, you know. If you want to talk about this, we can talk."

"I don't want to talk. I'm a man. Men don't have to talk about things," Nicky responded.

"It can't hurt."

"What do you know? You don't know anything. You certainly don't know me and what I want. How can you? How could you even begin...?" Will interrupted Nicky's venting with a kiss and Nicky stopped. How could he continue? Will tasted like honey and starburst. His skin smelled delicate yet strong- like soap on a rope. There was something about him that Nicky didn't understand, but the longer he stayed around him, the more he wanted to.

"You want to try this again?" Will asked.

"I don't want to talk about these things," Nicky said. "I mean, do we have to?"

"What's the harm? We've got time to kill. I'm presuming Donn didn't kill you in your sleep."

"No. But he is demanding a sacrifice of sorts."

"They all do. Something big and bad, I imagine." Will chuckled.

"Yeah. Something like that. I mean, there's always going to be big and bad things- but right now- Why am I thinking about you like this?"

"Like what?"

"Like in a sexy way. Like if I want to have you pierce me with your sword, I don't mean your katana. Is that normal?" Nicky said. "I've never felt this way before, if you know what I mean? I mean, there's always been attractions, but now I just..."

"You mean with another male presenting individual?" Will asked.

"Right. That. I mean, I've always defined myself as open, but I never really felt that kind of attraction and now..."

"Well, that's not unheard of. As a Fae, I am technically neither male nor female."

"You look pretty male to me. You might say you look excessively male at the moment."

"You like that?"

"I don't know. I've never thought of them, of that, like this—that—before." Nicky blushed. He wished he had more rubbing alcohol to drink. Will came close to him and played with his hands, reattaching Nicky's arm in the process and giving it an affectionate rub. Nicky didn't pull away this time. Partially because his hands would likely just stay where they were, and partially because he didn't want to leave. When Will stroked his arms, it felt like they were on fire, but in a good way. Like every touch was a torture of the best kind. "Do you still hate me?"

"Immeasurably. But I think I'm getting used to you." Will smiled. "I don't entirely hate you. I un-hate you. At least partially. For now."

"I am reassured," Nicky smirked, and Will pulled him closer. Nicky could feel Will squirm underneath him as he pressed his lips into Nicky's chest. The contrast in their bodies was arousing by itself, but just the way that Will seemed to effortlessly touch him was incredible. He wanted to know everything about him in a way he'd never felt with any woman before. When Will talked, he listened and sometimes, he actually tried to care about what was going on. For Nicky, that was immense progress. And the best part was that if Will ever pissed him off or did something awful, he could always just lock him back in the book for an extended period of time. He was sure Will would understand.

"You don't have to be anything," Will said as he lifted his head from Nicky for a second. "Neither of us has to be anything right now. Just relax and let me take you somewhere."

"Will I need to get changed?"

"I couldn't change you if I tried. And I don't want to try," Will responded. "But yes, you should probably wear some pants."

Chapter 41

THE CHAPTER WHERE THEY AMBUSH MOM

Like an amorous puppy, Nicky followed Will through the forest. Nicky carried his book. Will carried his pants. He seemed to be happy to be free from their tyrannical restrictions. Nicky wasn't about to argue.

As they walked, Nicky kept finding himself stealing a peek at Will's figure. Had he just been overcompensating all his life, or had his experiences with the Fae left him with more options than before? The idea was a curious one. In Will's own words, he was neither male nor female. And his mother had been so happy when she'd learned of his friend. And he did love Celine Dion, but in reality, who didn't? In his mind, all the pieces seemed to fit, but he didn't think they were the complete picture.

"Is it possible for someone to be both?" Nicky finally asked.

"Both what?"

"Both liking men and women?"

"Of course. Bisexuality in mortals is completely normal. In immortal creatures, it's almost a necessity. Sexuality is a different creature and there are many complicated and interesting aspects to it that can't be easily classified one way or the other. As it stands, I am technically both and neither and have taken both male and female mortal partners before. So you're nothing new to me."

"And an owl."

"Yes. And an owl," Will chuckled.

"How many?"

"Let's just say enough," Will said. "I've been alive for a while and Fae can be incredibly sexual creatures."

"I can tell. I was just thinking..."

"About what?"

"Are all fae this way? Like, is there some kind of sexy thing we can use against Donn?"

"It's possible. But his tastes are a bit more... complicated."

"Are you able to satisfy them?" Nicky asked. Will stopped and turned to Nicky with a confused look.

"You trying to pimp me out to Donn?"

"No," Nicky hesitated. "But I mean, if you're offering..." Will stepped closer to Nicky and looked down at him. Nicky suddenly remembered how much taller Will was. It was quite a shocking revelation. "It was a joke."

"Good. Keep it that way," Will sneered. Nicky forgot how disappointingly Will could look. "So what did he ask for, then?"

"He didn't say. Definitely something about killing or death. He just said it would be bad."

"Well then. I don't expect it will be a good thing."

"Yeah. But wouldn't that be great if it was?" Nicky said. "Do you really think my mom will know how to help us?"

"Maybe your dad left something behind. I figure it's worth a shot," Will said as they looked down the driveway to the small house. It was never picturesque, but in many ways Nicky found it homey. And it was undeniably comfortable. "Come on, let's go find out."

"Wait. I don't have to tell her anything about... you know... us? Will I?"

"I really don't care about that. But do what you want to do," Will responded. "Come on, let's go." They walked to the door and knocked. After a moment, she responded with a smile and a glass of wine in her hand.

"Oh, hello darlings! Nicky, three times in two days! Am I sick or something? Am I dying?" she chuckled to herself. "I'm just kidding. Come on, baby. We got lots of time for you."

"We?" Nicky asked.

"Oh yeah. An old friend of your father's stopped by. He's in the living room now." They entered, and looked over to see Donn sitting on a chair in the living room, although he didn't quite look the same as before. He wore a white jacket and had a much more pronounced gut than before. He almost looked as if he'd ate his other outfit and it had not gone down easily.

"Greetings gents. Pleasure to see you again," Donn said as a slimy smile pasted on his smug face.

"Nicky, I'll take your mom into the kitchen." Will said.

"For what, Sweetie? I don't mind staying here and talking. I love catching up with old friends. My, well, I haven't seen Drago in..."

"But I have so much to tell you about... something." Will looked at Nicky and shrugged. Nicky shook his head at him very distinctly.

"You don't need to tell her anything."

"What? Did you boys kill anyone?" his mom responded.

"Not today," Nicky responded.

"Surely she already knows everything she would need to know..." Will began.

"I mean, not everything," Nicky whispered.

"But Nicky, surely you told her what you would need to tell her," Will hissed. He was looking more like disapproving Will again. Nicky felt a pang of guilt worm its way around his guts.

Before anything else could happen, his mom floated over to Will with a titter, hooked him by the arm, and escorted him from the space.

"Oh, you boys are so fresh. Okay, Will. Let me make you boys a drink. Do you like vodka? I've got vodka. Also, if you need it mixed, then we might have some gin or something lighter. Also, we can play charades now because there's four of us! But first let me show you this new window treatment I got from Peruvia!" she droned on. Good, Nicky thought. That'll keep her safe.

Once they were out of earshot, Nicky turned to Donn and levelled his finger at him.

"You better not be planning to hurt her! "

"Hurt her? Hurt Linda? I would never hurt Linda. She's one of the few things we can all agree on. She's a peach."

"Yeah, she's peachy. So don't hurt her. Or I'll hurt you!"

"You're adorable. You couldn't hurt me if you tried."

"Well, I've got the book. I can use that on you!" Nicky said.

"You mean the book I created and infused with my own magic so that only I or a descendant of a very specific druid line could use it?" Donn said. "That book may have bonded with you, but it belongs to me. That book is me." To prove a point, he lifted up his hand, and the book appeared in it. Calmly, he then extended it back to Nicky, who took it and sheepishly placed it back in his pack.

"Fine," Nicky said. "So, why are you here? Are you here for me?"

"Not even a little bit. I wanted to see the man that she'd settled down with. You know the one. It's the one that you accidentally tore to pieces. He sure doesn't look worth the amount of effort to bring back again."

"He's not. I mean to me he's not. But to my mom... to my mom she likes him. Like really likes him."

"The way you like Will?"

"No. Not at all like that," Nicky stuttered. "Like in a real way."

"What you two have isn't real?"

"I'm not saying that. It's just new. There are a lot of new things happening with me and him and it's... new."

"I'm getting the sense that you're not sure about it yet. Very fair. Don't try to rush anything. Just let things happen. I mean, you've got all the time in the world to figure things out." Donn paused and looked at him with a smile. "Actually, there's a good chance that what I just told you was a lie."

"What do you want?"

"Well, as I said, blood magic requires great sacrifice. And this Bill person- horrid as it is- may just be able to be reassembled and delivered back to your mother. If you'd like that." Donn shrugged. "Not perfectly, mind you. Maybe a misplaced finger here. An extra organ there, but who's to say? Are you on board to get him back?"

Nicky bit his lip. "I am. Even if I meant I would have to see more of him." His voice was angry, and the words were heavy on his tongue.

"I don't think you'd have to worry about that," Donn said. "These things come at a price, you know."

"I know. You keep saying that."

"Well, this one might cost you more than you're willing to

pay," he said. "This deal costs you. As in, I'm going to take you."
Nicky paused for a moment and frowned.

"Okay. I hear what you're saying, and I now want to offer you three free rentals a week."

Chapter 42

The Chapter Where There's A Gaggle Of Women

"What'll it be, boy? Are you for this or is it no deal?" Donn asked. Nicky looked at him with a frown.

"Now, I don't know exactly why it has to be me. Couldn't we just kill a random homeless guy or something instead? Wouldn't that suffice?"

"First off, many homeless people are out there due to reasons that are not their fault, so you shouldn't treat them as disposable. Secondly, do you really think that a homeless person would offer to die so I could bring back someone they'd never met? Besides, who said anything about death? This is about you."

Nicky shrugged. He had a point, even if he didn't like it. "Okay. But why does it have to be me?"

"Blood demands blood. Death demands death. Him demands you. This is your request, so it best be your body that pays for it. You think you can pay the price?"

"But I don't want to die," Nicky whined.

"Then don't. This demands you, though, so this choice is all in your hands now. When you're ready, you know where to find me," Donn said as he sat on the pink chair that looked out over the front lawn.

"Here?" Nicky asked, pointing at the chair. "This is where you'll be?"

"Well, maybe up in the bedroom. I guess it depends how long you keep me waiting."

"Why would you be in the bedroom? You would just... oh." It took Nicky a moment, but he finally caught the intention. "I see."

Nicky wanted to smack Donn, but he had a funny feeling that would be a bad idea. He wanted to pummel Donn in the face, but figured that would be worse. Unsure what to do, he dug his hands into his pockets and went to the kitchen to see Will and his mom laughing over a cup of what looked like water, but knew it was more likely his mother's Wednesday special.

"Mom! Will! Things are happening."

"Oh. Love. Are you okay? You look flushed," his mom hic-cupped at him.

"I'm fine, mom!" Nicky's voice cracked and he could feel himself turning purple. "Will. Can I see you?"

Linda's face lit up for a moment as she surveyed the two of them.

"Wait... my mother sense is tingling..." she said as she waved her hands in the air like she was receiving radio signals. "My gaydar is off the charts right now. Are you two a thing? Is this a thing? Nicky, are you a thing now?" she gasped. To his surprise, she looked excited. Nicky turned to Will and crossed his arms.

"What did you tell her?" Nicky asked.

"Nothing! She's just excessively perceptive," Will retorted.

"Yeah. She can be that sometimes." Nicky shook his head. "I don't know, mom. There's a thing, but I don't know what that is yet."

"Well, good, baby. You can be whatever you want to be. As long as you lay off the cakes. You're getting a little bit more of a tummy," she said, poking Nicky in the midsection. Nicky flustered.

"Mom!" he said as he tried to knock her hand away.

"Oh, come off it, baby. Am I not allowed to poke you anymore, or is that just Will's territory now?"

"Oh my god, goodbye mom!" Nicky said as he grabbed Will's hand and dragged him out into the backyard. Will looked at him with a smirk. "What?"

"You're all flustered."

"Donn wants to kill me. Me. He wants me. I'm the prize." Will looked at him very seriously for a moment.

"I know this might sound like semantics, but did he say he wants your life, or that he wants you?" Will asked. Nicky blinked.

"Is there a difference?"

"With Fae there is. He wants your life means he wants to kill you. He wants you, well, that means... something else."

Nicky looked at him, unsure what he meant. And then he looked at him, knowing exactly what he meant. His eyes went wide. "Why would he want me?"

"Maybe he likes you. Maybe he just wants what I have. Maybe there's more here to discover. Could be any variety of things, but it seems like there might be a slightly more magical reason for this."

"Huh. First you, now him?" Nicky looked at Will. "Am I just irresistible?"

"Nope. Definitely not that," Will said as he ushered Nicky to the entrance by the arm. Nicky resisted and his arm popped off.

"I don't want to go back in there."

"We have to if we want to get to the front door," Will responded.

"But he's still there. He's in the chair. Leering at me like I'm a piece of meat."

"To him you are."

"Oh, man. Why couldn't he just want to kill me like everyone else?" Nicky groaned.

"That might be the case. But either way, we have to get out of this house."

"Fine. We get out of this house. And go somewhere. Where are we going?"

"At this point, I have no idea. Your home is out, the video store is out. You're responsible for the destruction of a strip club and a family animatronic diner."

"It's not my fault that my date was massive," Nicky spat. He suddenly looked at Will curiously. "Do you think Oberon was interested in me that way, too? How far do my charms proceed me?"

"Keep it in your pants, Casanova," Will said. "Step one. Get going."

"Okay. Fine," Nicky said. With a yank he opened the door to the kitchen, revealing a gathering of middle-aged women in various stages of debauchery. All of them were carrying a collection of rainbow flags and capes. Several were drinking their wines from penis straws.

"Happy coming out Nicky baby!" they all exclaimed.

"Oh my god, girls! Look at his face. He's so surprised!" his mom exclaimed as she came up and put a boa around his shoulders.

"Mom! Oh my god! What are you..." Nicky looked around

the room and could hardly find a space without a rainbow, a cupcake, glitter or cocaine. At least he hoped it was cocaine. "How on earth did you decorate all of this so quickly?"

"I just brought the girls over to celebrate this happy occasion." She gestured to Will, bringing him to the centre of the circle. "And this is his long time life partner, Will. I call him Willy because it's what my Nicky loves so much about him." Will flashed the ladies a smile.

"Ladies," Will beamed. They swooned.

"How does he feel? Oh, he looks like a statue. He's so handsome." A woman with big red hair stated.

"They make a cute couple," his mom said as she shoved him and Will together. "Look how Will makes Nicky look almost presentable. So handsome."

"Thanks mom. This has been awful. Now, if you ladies are done swooning, I've got work to do," Nicky said as he attempted to break away from the clingy cluster of chardonnay chuggers. It didn't work and soon he found his shoulder clung to by a conglomerate of bright pink press on nails.

"Nah, don't be silly Nicky. Come spend some more time with us! We've got so much to do." They heckled him. He was the pizza, and they were the swarm of manic seagulls.

"Come with me," Will said as he grabbed Nicky by the hand and pulled him through the kitchen. However, as was the case lately, whenever someone pulled a part of him, it split off. The ladies stopped and looked at the stump when Nicky got an idea. He began to scream. He screamed loud and long, and then the ladies joined in.

"Get the boy a band aid!" one of them called out. They all let go of him and Nicky quickly raced after Will until they were in the living room. Donn was still there, but this time was wearing a small rainbow bow tie. Nicky could've ran by when he paused and looked at Donn straight in his emerald eyes.

"When you said to me that you want me. You want to kill me, right?" Donn sucked on a cigar that Nicky was positive he didn't have a moment ago and grinned. He shivered. "Right. Thanks for clearing that up." Nicky followed Will outside. On the other side of the wall, screams could still be heard from the kitchen as the gaggle of women were now yelling at each other for being too loud.

"I'm guessing he didn't clear things up with you?"

"You're very astute," Nicky said. "Now let's go find a way to not have to fool around with a demon."

Chapter 43

The Chapter Where They Make A New Deal

"Can I maybe just wait in the car?" Nicky asked. Will tapped his foot on the gravel and he crossed his arms. He didn't look impressed. That looked more like the Will he was familiar with.

"You're the one who's going to have to do terrible things to someone if you don't play along."

"Okay. Okay," he said as he stood at the door. He didn't want to knock because he knew what was waiting for him on the other side. He stood and looked at it, hoping that somehow he could flash himself out of this situation. Sadly, there was no such luck. Clearing his throat, he looked back at Will, who gave him the 'go ahead already' look. Nicky pouted and knocked on the door.

"Come in," a voice called from the other side. The voice was smooth and succulent. He shivered slightly and opened the door. He stepped inside to be greeted by a wave of warmth and the smell of cinnamon and apples. It smelled delicious and he let the luxurious air wash over him. He looked around to see Titania standing in the buff over the stove.

"Naked!" Nicky called out and tried to avert his eyes when suddenly he found himself wondering what was happening. He looked back at Will and blushed harder as he walked into the room. "Don't look!"

"Hey Titania," he said, not caring.

"Hey Will. Grab a seat?"

"Yours?" he flirted. Titania giggled, and Nicky suddenly felt a twinge of jealousy burst from him. That was also a new feeling.

"Is something the matter, dear?" Titania asked, looking at Nicky breast first. Nicky began to shake.

"You're naked."

"Am I? I hardly noticed." She shrugged. "I find clothes just get in the way while you're baking so I try not to wear any. Frying is different. Then I always make sure to wear an apron." She wiggled, sending seductive ripples across her body. "See? Free and easy!" Nicky made a sound like a *harumph* and slunk into a chair, still trying not to look. "I see he let you out of the book."

"Yeah. Seems we've both come out."

"Come now, Will, you shouldn't use your lusty Fae magic on every mortal you come across," she said with a smile and Will shrugged.

"Didn't even need to use it this time. Turns out he just likes me."

"Well, he's not the smartest, so I can see that happening." She beamed at him before turning to Nicky with a smile. "You go, girl. You live that truth."

"You're still naked."

"But you're queer now. Surely my being naked doesn't bother you," she said as she walked over to Nicky and gave him a big hug. Nicky tried not to move for fear he would touch something he shouldn't. Then he did. Many times over.

"We need to talk to you about Donn."

"Vile man. I haven't slept with him in weeks," she said flippantly, before pausing. "Well, maybe days, but it's been a while.

Which is more than I could say for his stamina."

"You were sleeping with him while Oberon was locked away in the book?" Nicky asked.

"It's not like we're married or anything. I haven't seen him in, what, two hundred years? A woman is entitled to her own sexual desires, no?"

"I mean..." Nicky began, but wasn't sure what to say.

"Let me ask you plainly. Why are you asking me about Donn?"

"I was hoping you could help me. Defeat him. I think. I mean... he wants to use me for me, but I don't know if that means... you know... kinky things or he just wants to kill me."

"Well, knowing him, it could be both," Titania asked.

"So, Will here thought I should ask for your help. With either thing."

Titania leaned over to Nicky and grabbed his arm. "You want my help, you can have my help. But it'll cost you."

"What do you want?" Will asked.

"It's not me, is it? I don't want to be used for my body anymore. I'm delicate," Nicky said.

"Delicate like a rock." Will smirked.

"Stop it." He smacked Will's shoulder. "So very delicate."

Titania rolled her eyes. "I think I know a way I can help you out. But you might not like it."

"What is it?"

"What do you know about Excalibur?" she asked.

"The sword? Like the one that Arthur guy had?" he replied.

"Close enough. Truthfully, it wasn't originally Arthur's, but that's another matter. They said the sword had great value and great power. And that it was given to him boy..."

"The bitch in the bog!" Nicky cried out. Titania frowned at him.

"The lady in the lake," she over-enunciated in a very deliberate way. Just to make sure he caught her drift. Of which there was an overabundance available.

"What did I say?" Nicky asked. Will shook his head.

"She gave it to him because she assumed he was worthy, but apart from that, no one knows how I created the sword."

"You're the bitch?" Nicky asked.

"I'm the lady, got it?" Titania stated. "But that's not the point. The point is, the sword was made from Arthur's daughter. A sword of great power must come from the soul of someone who means the most to you."

"But I can't ask my mom to sacrifice herself and bring back Bill just to have him not be with her! And there's no one else I..." Nicky turned to Will, who smiled at him. "Oh, shit."

"Could a fae become a sword?" Will asked.

"I see no reason why not. It could be even more powerful and more dangerous than any sword before it."

"Then what are we waiting for? Let's do it. There's no time to waste." Will ushered but Nicky grabbed him by the shoulder and pulled him back.

"We can wait a little longer," Nicky said. "Maybe a lot longer than that if we need to."

"But every minute we wait, you get further from getting your mom's boyfriend back."

"But I don't think I want to lose you," Nicky said. "I think I like, I mean, I like being around you and..." Will put his finger to Nicky's lips and smiled warmly at him.

"You want to go have sex before this happens?"

"I'll follow you."

Chapter 44

THE CHAPTER WHERE THEY HAVE A HEART TO HEART

"I'm not sure I want you to do this," Nicky said. He wasn't sure if Will had known he was there, but he didn't look surprised.

"I don't think you have a choice in the matter. You won't be able to defeat him by yourself." Will held up his hand and smiled as he weaved his fingers between Nicky's. Nicky hesitated. Will's hands felt warm and strong. Not like his doughy stumpy fingers. Will was always graceful and elegant in everything. He was not.

"Maybe I don't have to defeat him. Maybe I can just..."

"There's nothing you can do. It's come to this. Tonight he will come and collect on his debt and you will have to go with him. Unless you fight him."

"But then I'll die."

"Not if I'm in your hands," Will said. "Let her make me your sword, and I'll do everything I can to protect you. Your hands are fairly autonomous at this point, anyway. They'll fight practically by themselves."

"But then... you'll be gone."

"Not gone. I'll be in your hands. Heck, I'll *be* your hands." Will smiled at him.

"But you won't be... you. You won't be yourself anymore.

You'll be a sword."

"Yes. That is the idea."

"And you're okay with that?"

"If it's to protect you, then yes. I'll do it," Will said. "It'll feel good knowing that you're the one I'll be protecting. I'll keep you safe and you keep me in good condition." Will grabbed Nicky's hands and held them up before kissing his knuckles. Nicky wanted to pull away, but he could feel his heart melting as he felt Will. He knew in the back of his head that this would be one of the last times he'd feel Will this way, and he didn't want it to end.

"Typical," Nicky said. "Just when I start to like someone, they get turned into an inanimate object."

"Are you saying you like me?"

"I think that should be fairly obvious by now. So will you be able to still think and stuff? Will you be able to do anything?" Nicky asked. Will shrugged.

"I don't know. I've never been a sword before. Just locked inside a book."

"Right," Nicky said as he smiled. He wasn't sure why he was smiling. Maybe it was because he was hoping that a smile would force the tears to roll back into his brain, or however tears worked. "I am sorry about that."

"Not your fault. You only did it to me twice," he said.

Nicky shrugged. "So... If this is the last time I get you while you're corporeal..." he said.

Will raised his eyebrow and smirked. "Best make it count, then."

After a rigorous few minutes of intimacy, Nicky was laying in the arms of Will. His brain was a mess of confusion.

"Why would you do this for me?" Nicky asked.

"Because..." was all he said. Neither said anything else.

They knew when they left this space that Titania would be there to do whatever magic she would do to get Will to become a sword. And then he'd have to go off and save the world. But in this moment, somehow he couldn't help but feel like he was losing a part of his.

Chapter 45

THE CHAPTER WHERE THEY COMPROMISE

So Nicky sat between Titania and Will and for a moment there, they were going to go through with it. But then Nicky had a change of heart.

"Now, I know what you said. That it had to be an act of ultimate sacrifice from someone. But what if that sacrifice didn't need to come from love, but could come from hate?"

"I think that's a stupid idea." Titania frowned.

"But, what if it could be? I have an idea."

"Oh, no," Will began, but Nicky cut him off.

"I have this book, right. And inside there is someone who hates me. Like really hates me. What if we could use that strong emotion as the anchor instead of love?"

"It's a dumb idea," Titania dismissed.

"But it's worth trying, no?" Nicky asked.

"No," Titania chuckled to herself. "Who were you thinking of using, anyway?"

"Oberon?" This pricked her interest.

"Oberon. You want me to use my husband..."

"I thought he was your ex-husband?" Will asked.

"My on and off again husband, as a magic sword for you to fight Donn with?"

"Yes. Exactly that. What do you think?"

Titania pondered. "The idea... I hate to say it—the idea has merit."

"That sounds good."

"But why on earth do you think that Oberon would agree to this?" Titania asked.

"We could ask him?" Nicky replied. "I can take him out of the book and we could find out what he would like to do." Before either could protest, he opened the book and within moments Oberon was sat before them.

"Hi," Nicky said, breaking the awkward silence. Oberon frowned at him and picked a clump of black goo off of his hair.

"Why am I here?" Oberon asked. He sounded grumpy.

"I want to ask you something, and I want you to hear me out on this. Okay?" Oberon leered at him. "Would you want to become a sword for me so I can defeat an evil god of death?"

Oberon raised an eyebrow before turning to Titania.

"Really?" he asked. She shrugged. "Obviously not."

"Can you give me one good reason why not?" she replied.

"For one, I don't like the idea of helping you," Oberon sneered.

"Granted."

"Also, I don't want to be an inanimate piece of metal for an age."

"I could turn you back after a time," Titania said. "But it would show tremendous dedication if you did do it."

"Dedication to what?" Oberon jeered.

"To me! This little snot has been with Will for less time than a celebrity marriage and he's already got him wanting to be a sword for him. And you've known me for how many aeons and you wouldn't do this for me?" Oberon appeared stunned.

"You want me to... you want me to become a sword? Why on Earth..."

"Because it would show me that you cared. You do care, don't you?"

Oberon stuttered something inconclusive.

"This got weird," Will whispered to Nicky, who only nodded in response.

"You want me to show my love for you, by becoming a sword for the man I hate?"

"Yes," she said. "Do this for me. Put me ahead of your battles, and your drama, and your daddy issues. Let me make you into this tool and I'll love you more than you ever knew was possible."

Oberon looked from Titania to Nicky, then back to her.

"If this is what you want and... I suppose I can. I can do this for you."

Titania smiled. And lifted a velvet blanket off the bed. She draped it over Oberon's head and, with a flourish, he was gone.

All that remained on the chair was a long purple dildo that flopped. Taking it, she handed it over to Nicky with a smile.

"Be careful with this. I want to ensure I can use it after."

Then, with the dildo in one hand and Will's hand in the other, they left.

Chapter 46

THE CHAPTER WHERE THEY PREPARE FOR THE BIG BAD

Metal. It was all very metal.

Thunder cracked the sky as Nicky stood with the dildo flopping in his hand. It had been Oberon, and Nicky could feel the burly mans energy pulsing around it. With every flop, he knew what was held within it. It was a very strange feeling.

He held it up as the storm around him surged and the rain poured down. It was so heavy and thick and flapped in the wind. His eyes felt like they were on fire and the rocky ground around him felt weak and unsteady, as if the world around him was slowly coming apart at the seams. Bursts of golden and green fire splashed around him as small bits of fiery earth surged down from the sky like meteorites. It was all very metal.

Gripping the hilt of the toy with both hands, Nicky bent his legs. He had held it like a sword and could feel Oberon's energy guiding him. He backed up, looking up, eager for any sign that what he was waiting for would appear.

"You're doing fine Nicky. Just stay low. Wait. Just wait." He could hear the voice calling from behind him.

"I'm not going to win. I don't want to fight him," Nicky said under his breath.

"You have to. You got yourself into this. You'll get yourself out." He squeezed the weapon tighter. He turned to see Will beside him unsheathe his sword and smiled at him.

A lightning blast obliterated a small tree beside him, which instantly landed on Will. Nicky looked over just in time to see him on the ground unconscious when he felt himself get pummelled in the stomach. Nicky flew back and landed with a heavy thump. Coughing, he curled up, looking to see the body of a huge man. His arms were long and scaly and his face looked like a smashed lizard. His body was thick with muscle and he had two heads atop his mighty frame. His eyes pierced him and Nicky could feel a pit of dread opening in his stomach.

"Oh lord. Will! Will are you okay?" Will looked up and raised his thumb, but didn't get up. As he did, Donn, or whatever the creature was that lumbered towards him, pelted Will with a clump of dirt and Will fell to the ground again.

"We don't have to do this!" Nicky exclaimed.

The giant creature blinked at him.

"Oh. But we do," the creature hissed. "You want me to bring that man back, that demands the body."

"My body is not on the table!" Nicky cried out.

"You backed out of our deal," Donn said. His twin voices unified. Nicky gripped the dildo and hoped his hands would stay on as he lifted it into the sky. "For that, there is a punishment."

"You didn't fulfil your side of the bargain!"

"I did. I brought him back. In fact, I'm bringing him back right now. You should have reassembled him first. He can't survive as a pile. You should have thought that through! Now you will be mine!"

"You lie. I know you can. You just didn't want to. You chickened out."

"That's not the case at all, boyo. You got me all wrong. Maybe you overestimate my power."

"And maybe you underestimate my intelligence!" Nicky exclaimed as he brought the dildo down in an arch, trying to chop it through Donn's skull. Donn, however, was expecting this and lifted his mighty arm, blocking Nicky from his attack. He gripped the dildo in his bare hand and it squeaked like a dog toy. He tossed it away like it was nothing.

"You don't stand a chance, boyo. Surrender and I'll take you to my dungeon."

"You'll lock me away forever?"

"Not that kind of dungeon, boyo." Donn said as a creepy smile spread across his face. He licked his fat lips in a mocking way. Nicky shuddered. He ran over to his weapon and levelled it at Donn.

"Take another step and I'll plough this through your heart!" Nicky exclaimed, but Donn just smiled. "Or maybe something else. I can get creative here."

"You ain't got the stones," he replied, to which Nicky yelled and grabbed the weapon and swung again.

"You mean these stones?" Nicky responded as he knelt down and grabbed a handful of dirt, and sprayed it into Donn's eyes. Donn screamed and Nicky took the dildo and rammed it into the mouth on one of Donn's heads.

They then looked at each other before glaring at Nicky and frowned. He removed the toy from his mouth and threw it to the side, this time landing beside Will.

"You idiot. Without me, you'll never get him back."

"I'll find a way," Nicky replied. "Or you can bring him back now. I know that a single weapon isn't enough to kill you. But it's a start!"

Nicky ran over to the dildo and gripped it in his hands. With a yell, he summoned his courage and prepared himself for a grand battle.

Chapter 47

THE CHAPTER WHERE THEY BATTLE

A grand battle ensued. It was awesome.

Chapter 48

THE CHAPTER WHERE THE BATTLE IS OVER

Donn sat in a chair opposite Nicky as the two of them shared some cheesy fries.

"For a mortal, you fought nobly," Donn said.

"Thanks. For an immortal war god, you did good yourself."

"You still lost, of course."

"Of course. I went up against an eldritch god. I guess the concept of me winning would be impossible, really."

"Yes. I would have crushed you like a bug."

They shared a laugh, and Will came to the table. He was carrying cheesy fries. He did not appear to be overly happy.

"How you managed to dodge that building I threw at you and then fire your weapon with such precise aim, I will never know. I swear you embedded that thing in so far, I thought I'd need to have a doctor dig it out."

Nicky couldn't know for sure, but he swore he could feel Oberon shudder from within the contraption.

"Yeah... that was quite the adventure." Nicky laughed. He relaxed a bit. The battle had been truly epic, but now that they were on the other side of it and he had definitively lost. He had fought nobly and still come up with nothing.

"If you'll excuse me just a moment, I think I'll go and destroy this bathroom." Donn said as he got up, tipped his hat to the boys, and stepped away.

"You look upset," Will broke the silence.

"I am," Nicky responded. "I lost."

"Yeah, well, you did better than me. I lasted what... thirty seconds?"

"Maybe." Nicky slouched back into the polyester chair. "I had just hoped..."

"Dumb luck can only take you so far," Will responded. "And come on, you were up against impossible odds."

"But I liked those odds," Nicky said as a sound of smashing porcelain filled the diner. Apparently Donn was serious with what he had said. As a barrage of screams and confusion washed over the space, Will reached across the table and grabbed Nicky's hand.

"You did good."

"But I failed," Nicky responded. "I just wanted to bring Bill back and I couldn't."

"Yeah... I mean there is that too..." Will responded. "What're you going to tell your mom?"

"I don't know. I guess the truth."

"Well good. The truth seems like a good place to start," Will said. "But first, have your disgusting cheese fries, and let's get you back to your place to take a shower."

Chapter 49

THE CHAPTER WHERE HE TALKS TO A SWORD

Nicky laid back on the couch, feeling some combination of remorse, frustration and relief. Also, with Will in the shower, the lights flickered constantly, and for the first time, Nicky wondered if his death trap of an apartment might also be a fire hazard.

"I mean, it's not like I don't want to try. I just wish I knew what they wanted." Nicky said, as he motioned to Oberon. "I mean, I just wish I could take it like I..."

"Hey, um... Nicky?" a voice called from the doorway.

"Teddy?" Nicky looked up to see Teddy standing in the doorway. He still resembled tapioca made flesh, but at least he appeared to still be human. "Hi."

"Hi," Teddy replied.

"What're you doing here?"

"I just delivered your mail. Lots of bills." Teddy shrugged.. "Is, uh... that yours?" Teddy asked, pointing to the Oberon dildo.

"Yeah. What about it?"

"Were you, uh..." Teddy looked around as if trying to figure out what to say. "Were you just talking to it?"

"More like talking at it. It's not saying anything back."

"Right. well, I mean you know it is a ... toy, right?" Teddy sounded concerned.

"Yeah? What about it?"

"Nothing. I, uh... forget I said anything." Teddy awkwardly started to walk away when he paused. "Hey, man?"

"What's up?"

"Did you want to hang out sometime? I mean, I know it's been a while, but lately things have just been really weird and I could really use a friend right now. Think you could help me out?" He looked at Nicky and smirked. "I can bring some weed and pizza if you can rent us a movie." Nicky just shrugged.

"Yeah. Sure, man. Whatever floats your boat."

"Cool. I'll come by tonight. And uh, man?"

"What?" Nicky asked.

"Maybe don't yell at your sex toys. They've got feelings too." Teddy waved and started to walk away when Nicky walked up to the dildo and decided that maybe putting it away would be a good idea. Titania had said that she wanted it after he was done, but he had no idea when that would be.

"Nicky?" A voice came from behind him, and in a panic, Nicky reacted. Not wanting to be seen with the apparatus, he flung it behind him, not realising that was where the voice had come from. When he turned to the door, an equal mix of terror and regret, he was surprised to see a very familiar shape in the front doorway with the dildo plunged firmly into his chest.

"Damn. That nearly got me," Bill said as he staggered into the space. Nicky looked down to see the contraption very clearly running straight through him. Nicky paused.

"It... It is straight through you," Nicky said, pointing to Bill's chest. Bill looked down at him and paused. He looked up at Nicky and smiled.

"Well, so it is. No hard feelings then."

"Should... should I take you to the hospital?" Nicky asked. Bill just laughed.

"Boyo, there's no need. I'm not truly alive anyway." Bill chuckled to himself. "Oh, the horrors I've seen. What say we head home and get a nice glass of milk?"

"Sure. I mean, if you think you can with the thing and all."

"Oh, of course I can. If Donn has cursed me with this hellish half life, the best I can do is ensure that you're keeping safe. Now come on, let's go get this taken care of."

"Okay. I just... Mom will be so happy."

"I love her very much you know," Bill said as he wrapped Nicky in a hug. Nicky didn't fight it.

"I know," Nicky responded. "I'm sorry I killed you."

"I know," Bill responded. "Now, let's get going. I'm sure your mom will have some questions for me when we get back there."

Chapter 50

THE CHAPTER WHERE HIS MOM SAYS SOMETHING

Nicky hovered by the phone. Nicky knew that she wasn't likely to pick up. It was noon on a Sunday. Bill had been back for a week now, and the two of them seemed fine. Nicky was actually able to spend time with them. Not a lot, they were still family, after all, but some.

And then she called him.

"Hello?"

"Hi. Mom. It's me."

"Oh, hey baby! You coming over today? I mowed the grass last night. You should see it! It's all green now!"

"That's great, Mom, but that's not why I'm calling. I want to talk to you about something."

"Is it you being a queer?" She pronounced queer with three syllables. "You know you can always talk to me about you being gay, or bi-sesh-ually anytime. You know I had a fling once with this girl and I'm not going to say it was steamy, but it was really nice! I had a great time and I know that you've been going through some stuff and it's..."

"No mom. It's about Bill. Do you want me to come over and we can talk about this or would you rather-"

"Nicky. I know everything. I'm like a psychic. It's like I've got a fifth sense or something. How did you think I had that cake ready for you so fast?" She said.

"What cake?"

"Oh, nevermind. I ate it before you got here. It was supposed to be a coming out cake. But I guess it came out too early!" she howled. "Look, why don't I come over there and we can have a heart to heart and I'll tell you all about your family tree, okay? I think maybe it's time that you know the truth, okay, baby? Just maybe kick your friend out of the bed first so I have space to sit. And I'll grab some coffee on the way, okay? That okay baby?"

"Yeah, Mom, that sounds great," Nicky said as he turned towards the bedroom to see Will sleeping on it. He smiled and closed the door. No sense in interrupting his sleep.

Then he turned around and saw his mom standing in the doorway with donuts.

"How did you...?"

"Psychic remember? Plus, I was calling you from my new cell phone. Look." She showed it to him. It was as big as she was.

"Oh, don't worry. I knew you would. Now shove over. I've brought donuts," she said as she set them down in front of him. Nicky took one and thanked his mother as she sat next to him and smiled. She put her hand on his cheek affectionately and stroked his hair. "So young. So dumb. But you did okay. Not great, but okay."

"What do you mean?"

"With your mission. I mean, normally we don't even open the book and have to find a way to have the book fall open, but you just opened it right away. Like a good, natural, stupid son. Like the best kind of good natured, stupid son. But then, once you actually got out there and started fighting them, you weren't awful. You got a few good hits in there, after all."

"This whole thing was a setup?" Nicky asked.

"Of course, baby. What? You don't think magic books just fall into anyone's laps, do you? You were being tested. By me."

"But why?"

"Because it was time. We can't have you just working in a video store until you're old and dying, can we?" she asked. "This way you get to know what you really are and what you're doing. You should have seen your father before his mission. He actually thought that he could have a career as a slam poet. I mean, he could've. But he was terrible at it."

"So... you made me queer?"

"No dear. That's all you. And if you are, I don't care. Fae are neither men nor women. They just get attached to you. Like being a part of your body until your hand falls off. Something like that, yeah?"

"So, I guess I'm just this way now."

"Something like that. But you really always were this way. And Bill is really dead even though he's undead and I'm okay with that. That's not your fault. It's mine for not laying armour in his sweater vests despite his protestations. I knew I should have."

"You know he was with Titania that night, right?"

"Not his fault. She's a very sexy woman. I should know. I spent some time with her in college and her bosoms were..."

"Like giant water beds."

"You too, eh? She's the best," she said, as she took a large chug of wine. "But you know, if she made him a sword, I might be able to do something about that." Nicky's eyes widened, and he gave his mom a hug. "Nicky stop. Mommy can't spill her wine. If she does, you get nothing. Now come on, let's leave before Will wakes up."

Chapter 51

THE CHAPTER WHERE THINGS CONTINUE

With his mother a few paces behind him, Nicky continued his walk deep into the forest. It felt strange to be here with his mom, but what really creeped him out was how quiet she was being. He couldn't remember the last time he had spent with his mother where she hadn't been talking the entire time, but here, walking through the woods, she was absolutely silent.

"How nice to see you again," Donn said as he appeared from the woods. "I trust you've come to return the book." Nicky didn't say anything and simply reached into the bag, grabbed the book, and handed it over to Donn.

"So you do this every generation?"

"Since the one you call Keith," Donn replied. "Sure, I've changed a lot since then. We've learned. We've adapted. But to every boy in the bloodline, we will test them." Nicky frowned.

"So, what will you do now?" Nicky asked.

"What do you mean?" Donn retorted.

"I'm the end of the bloodline. I mean, I'm with Will. How can I have an heir when I won't have any kids?"

A sneaky smile slid across Donn's face. "Oh. We have ways," he said, poking Nicky in his slightly doughy belly and turning away. "I'll be seeing you soon, Nicky. Be prepared."

Nicky turned to his mother with a look of concern.

"Oh, don't worry about that. He won't be back unless this book sells like hot cakes. You've got nothing to worry about."

"But how do you..."

"Psychic remember?" his mom said, and smiled. "Don't worry. It'll be fine. You'll be fine. You'll go home, cuddle up with your boyfriend, and you likely won't get pregnant."

"See, now I am concerned. Is this a thing? Should I be concerned?" Nicky's mom just smiled and began to walk away.

"Come on, boy. We've got church in two hours, and I need to do my hair."

That night, Nicky, Teddy and Will were all sitting on the couch playing video games and having a comfortable time. There was beer and pizza on the table, and the front door actually closed now. Nicky felt comfortable around Will in a way that was fresh, and new- and nice in a way that made him not want to constantly imprison him in a semi-sentient book.

They had prepared themselves for company. What they had not prepared themselves for was Vinny.

Bursting into the room, looking dishevelled and unkempt, Vinny rocketed into the space, smiling.

"She's back! I found her! She's returned to me!" Vinny was practically singing.

"Vinny? You're alive?" Will asked.

"I thought you said he was fine," Nicky quipped at Will.

"He's been gone for a week and... you know what, yes. He's fine." Will paused. "As I knew he would be."

"Where have you been?" Nicky asked.

"Out. Searching. Looking. And now I have found her!" Vinny

responded as he held the door open for a beautiful fish woman to walk in.

"Hello," she cooed.

"Gurgles?" Nicky asked.

"Gurglana actually." She corrected him.

"I've been looking for her. Scouring the woods for any trace of her. But then I found a guy with a hat and he helped me find her and now she's back." Nicky and Will shared a look of concern, but neither saw any hideous wounds on his neck, so they didn't say anything.

"Well... Good. Good for you," Nicky said as he took a sip of beer.

"Um... are you a fish woman?" Teddy finally asked.

"No," Vinny said. "She's... Albanian."

"Ah," Teddy responded. "Nice to meet you."

Nicky chuckled to himself. Like anyone would ever believe there was a place called Albania.

"Did you... want to play video games?" Nicky asked, holding the controller out to the odd couple. Gurglana snapped it out of his hands, sat beside him, and grabbed a beer.

"I'm playing as Peach," she exclaimed.

It was comfortable. It was night, and everyone had left. Nicky was getting used to having Will around. For one, he actually made the place feel liveable. He did little things like repair things that broke, laundry, and even scrubbed the toilet. His space felt less like a hovel every day, and he was okay with that.

That night they slid into bed together and wrapped their arms into a knot, which was something Nicky was very good at considering they were detachable, and kissed.

"I'm glad you're not a sword."

"Me too," Will responded.

"When do you think Titania will be by for her... you know?"

"Maybe she never will be." Will shrugged.

"You think he's watching us?"

"Absolutely," Will said as he began to glow. Small orbs of light radiated off of him as he brought his lips closed to Nicky's. "We can give him a good show."

Nicky smiled as they kissed again. Right now, he felt safe and sound in the arms of the fae who loved him. He knew that right now everything would be good, at least until they weren't.

And then everything went wrong.

But that's for the next book.

Acknowledgements

First off, big thanks to my family for raising me on humour.

My friends, for putting up with me. Andrew and the team at Spectrum for both your patience, support and encouragement through this process. Been an honour!

The readers for this book: especially Jacob who always is willing to take a look at the things I write. Susan, who always loves to support what I make. Glen who eternally supports - and all my test readers who I brought jokes to through the piece.

This book has been an Everest, and now it's out. And that's awesome.

About the Author

Matti McLean is a multidisciplinary artist and writer working in Toronto, Ontario.

As a creator he has healmed several creative projects including the body painting project "The Human Canvas Initiative" and the production of several theatrical productions throughout Toronto and Ontario. He is currently creating art which is then printed on clothing as a part of his clothing company "One Chic Geek".

As an author, he has two published books "Catalyst" and "The Cypher"- and has produced hundreds of monologues as a part of his "20/20" and Matti Monologue initiatives.

He is thrilled to be a part of the team at Spectrum Books and is eager to be able to share his passions, humour and quirky sensibilities with the world.

Excellent LGBTQ+ fiction by unique, wonderful authors.
Thrillers
Mystery
Romance
Young Adult
& More

Join our mailing list here for news, offers and free books!

Visit our website for more Spectrum Books
www.spectrum-books.com

Or find us on Instagram
@spectrumbookpublisher

www.ingramcontent.com/pod-product-compliance
Lightning Source LLC
Chambersburg PA
CBHW050728180626
46814CB00002B/657